SHIFU, YOU'LL DO ANYTHING FOR A LAUGH

Also by Mo Yan

The Garlic Ballads
The Republic of Wine
Big Breasts and Wide Hips
Life and Death Are Wearing Me Out

SHIFU, YOU'LL DO ANYTHING FOR A LAUGH

MO YAN

Translated from the Chinese
by Howard Goldblatt

ARCADE PUBLISHING • NEW YORK

Arcade Publishing books may be purchased in bulk at special discounts for sales promotion, corporate gifts, fund-raising, or educational purposes. Special editions can also be created to specifications. For details, contact the Special Sales Department, Arcade Publishing, 307 West 36th Street, 11th Floor, New York, NY 10018 or arcade@skyhorsepublishing.com.

Arcade Publishing® is a registered trademark of Skyhorse Publishing, Inc.®, a Delaware corporation.

Visit our website at www.arcadepub.com.

10 9 8 7 6 5 4 3 2 1

Library of Congress Cataloging-in-Publication Data is available on file.

ISBN: 978-1-61145-735-3

Printed in the United States of America

Contents

SHIFU, YOU'LL DO ANYTHING FOR A LAUGH

Preface

Hunger and Loneliness: My Muses

EVERY PERSON HAS HIS OWN REASONS FOR BECOMING A WRITER, AND I am no exception. But why I became the sort of writer I am and not another Hemingway or Faulkner is, I believe, linked to my childhood experiences. They have been a boon to my writing career and are what will make it possible for me to keep at it down the road.

Looking back some forty years, to the early 1960s, I revisit one of modern China's most bizarre periods, an era of unprecedented fanaticism. On one hand, those years saw the country in the grips of economic stagnation and individual deprivation. The people struggled to keep death from their door, with little to eat and rags for clothes; on the other hand, it was a time of intense political passions, when starving citizens tightened their belts and followed the Party in its Communist experiment. We may have been famished at the time, but we considered ourselves to be the luckiest people in the world. Two-thirds of the world's people, we believed, were living in dire misery, and it was our sacred duty to rescue them from the sea of suffering in which they were drowning. It wasn't until the 1980s, when China opened its door to the outside world, that we finally began to face reality, as if waking from a dream.

As a child, I knew nothing about photography, and even if I had I couldn't have afforded to have my picture taken. So I am able to piece together an image of my childhood based solely upon historical photographs and my own recollections, although I daresay that the image I conjure up is real to me. Back then, five- or six-year-olds like myself went virtually naked all through the spring, the summer, and the fall. We threw something over our backs only during the bitterly cold winters. Such tattered clothes are beyond the imagination of today's children in China. My grandmother once told me that while there is no suffering a person cannot endure, there is plenty of good fortune one can never hope to enjoy. I believe that. I also believe in Darwin's theory of the survival of the fittest. When someone is thrown into the most perilous circumstances, he may well display surprising vitality. Those who cannot adapt die off, while those who survive are of the best stock. So I guess I can say I come from superior stock. During those times, we had an amazing ability to withstand cold. With our bottoms exposed, we didn't feel that the cold was unbearable, even though feathered birds cried in the freezing weather. If you had come to our village back then, you'd have seen plenty of children with their bottoms exposed or wearing only a bit of thin clothing as they chased each other in the snow, having a wonderful, rowdy time. I have nothing but admiration for myself as a youngster; I was a force to be reckoned with then, a much finer specimen than I am now. As kids, we had little meat on our bones; we were sticklike figures with big rounded bellies, the skin stretched so taut it was nearly transparent — you could just about see our intestines twist and coil on the other side. Our necks were so long and thin it was a miracle they could support our heavy heads.

And what ran through those heads was simplicity itself: all we ever thought about was food and how to get it. We were like a pack of starving dogs, haunting the streets and lanes sniffing the air for something to put inside our bellies. Plenty of things no one would even consider putting into their mouths these days were treats for us then. We ate the leaves off trees, and once they were gone we turned our attention to the bark. After that, we gnawed on the trunks themselves. No trees in the world ever suffered as much as those in our village. But instead of wearing our teeth down, our peculiar diet made them as sharp and strong as knives. Nothing could stand up to them. One of my childhood friends became an electrician after he grew up. There were no pliers or knives in his tool kit; all he needed was his teeth to bite through wire as thick as a pencil — those were the tools of his trade. I had strong teeth too, but not as strong as my electrician friend's. Otherwise, I might have become a first-rate electrician rather than a writer.

In the spring of 1961, a load of glistening coal was delivered to our elementary school. We were so out of touch we didn't know what the stuff was. But one of the brighter kids picked up a piece, bit off a chunk, and started crunching away. The look of near rapture on his face meant it must have been delicious, so we rushed over, grabbed pieces of our own, and started crunching away. The more I ate, the better the stuff tasted, until it seemed absolutely delicious. Then some of the village adults who were looking on came up to see what we were eating with such gusto, and joined in. When the principal came out to put a stop to this feast, that only led to pushing and shoving. Just what that coal felt like down in my belly is something I can no longer recall, but I'll never forget how it tasted. Don't for a minute think there was no pleasure in our lives back then. We had fun doing lots of things. Topping the list of fun things to do was gleefully eating something we'd never considered food before.

The famine lasted for a couple of years or more, until the mid-1960s, when life improved. We still didn't have enough to eat, but every person was allotted about 200 pounds of grain per year; that combined with the wild greens we foraged in the fields was enough to get by on, and fewer people starved to death.

Obviously, the experience of going hungry cannot, by itself, make a writer out of someone, but once I became a writer, I had a deeper understanding of life than most because of it. Prolonged hunger made me realize how very important food is to people. Glory, causes, careers, and love mean nothing on an empty stomach. Because of food, I lost my self-respect; because of food, I suffered the humiliation of a lowly cur; and because of food I took up creative writing, with a vengeance.

After becoming a writer, I began to think back to the loneliness of my childhood, much the same as I thought back to my experience of going hungry every time I sat at a table piled high with good food. The place where I was born, Northeast Gaomi Township, is situated at a spot where three counties converge. It's a vast, sparsely populated area that lacks adequate transportation. As far as the eye can see, my village is surrounded by weed-covered, low-lying land topped by wildflowers. I had been taken out of school at a very young age, so while other kids were sitting in classrooms, I was taking cattle out into the field to graze. Eventually, I got to know more about cattle than I did about people. I knew what made them happy, angry, sad, and content; I knew what their expressions meant; and I knew what they were thinking. On that vast stretch of uncultivated land it was just me and a few head of cattle. They grazed calmly, their eyes appearing as blue as the ocean. When I tried to talk to them, they ignored me, caring only about the tasty grass on the ground. So I'd lie on my back and watch puffy clouds drift slowly across the sky, pretending they were a bunch of big, lazy men. But when I tried to talk to them, they ignored me too. There were lots of birds up in the sky — meadowlarks, common larks, and other familiar types I couldn't name. Their calls moved me deeply, often to the point of tears. I tried talking to them too, but they were much too busy to pay any attention to me. So I lay there in the grass feeling sad, and began to let my imagination run wild. In my dreamy state of mind, all sorts of wonderful thoughts poured into my head, helping me gain an understanding of love and decency.

Pretty soon I learned how to talk to myself. I developed uncommon gifts of expression, able to talk on and on not only with eloquence but even in rhyme. My mother once overheard me talking to a tree. Alarmed, she said to my father, "Father of our son, do you think there's something wrong with him?" Later, when I was old enough, I entered adult society as a member of a labor brigade, and the habit of talking to myself that had begun when I was tending cattle caused nothing but trouble in my family. "Son," my mother pleaded with me, "don't you ever stop talking?" Moved to tears by the look on face, I promised I'd stop. But the minute there were people around, out came all the words I'd stored up inside, like rats fleeing a nest. That would be followed by powerful feelings of remorse and an overwhelming sense that I had once again failed to take my mother's instructions to heart. That's why I chose Mo Yan — Don't Speak — as a pen name. But as my exasperated mother so often said, "A dog can't keep from eating excrement, and a wolf can't stop from eating meat." I simply couldn't stop talking. It's a habit that has caused me to offend many of my fellow writers, because what invariably comes out of my mouth is the unvarnished truth. Now that I'm well into my middle years, the words have begun to taper off, which must come as a comfort to my mother's spirit as it looks down on me.

My dream of becoming a writer was formed early on, back when one of my neighbors, a college student majoring in Chinese, was labeled a rightist, kicked out of school, and sent back to the countryside to work in the fields. We labored side by side. At first he couldn't forget he'd been a college student, as his elegant way of speaking and refined manners made clear. But the rigors of country living and the backbreaking labor quickly stripped away every vestige of his intellectual background, and he became a common peasant, just like me. During breaks out in the field, when our grumbling stomachs sent a sour taste up into our mouths, our greatest entertainment was talking among ourselves about food. We, along with some of the other field hands, would trade descriptions of delicious foods we had eaten or heard about. It was truly food for the soul. The speakers would invariably have us all drooling.

One old-timer talked about all the famous dishes he had

seen as a waiter in a Qingdao restaurant: braised beef tournedos, pan-fried chicken, things like that. Wide-eyed, we stared at his mouth until we could smell the aroma of all that delicious food and see it materialize, as if it had dropped from the sky. The "rightist" student said he knew someone who had written a book that brought him thousands, maybe tens of thousands, in royalties. Each and every day the fellow ate *jiaozi*, those tasty little pork dumplings, at all three meals, the oil oozing from inside with each bite. When we said we didn't believe anyone could be so rich as to eat *jiaozi* three times a day, the former student said scornfully, "He's a writer, for goodness sake! You understand? A writer!" That's all I needed to know: become a writer and you can eat meaty *jiaozi* three times a day. Life doesn't get any better than that. Why, not even the gods could do better. That's when I made up my mind to become a writer someday.

When I started out, noble ambitions were the furthest thing from my mind. Unlike so many of my peers, who saw themselves as "engineers of the soul," I didn't give a damn about improving society through fiction. As I've said, my motivation was quite primitive: I had a longing to eat good food. To be sure, after gaining a bit of a reputation, I learned the art of high-sounding utterances, but they were so hollow, even I didn't believe them. Owing to my lower-class background, the stories I wrote were filled with the commonest of views, and anyone looking for traces of elegance or graceful beauty in them would likely come away disappointed. There's nothing I can do about that. A writer writes what he knows, in ways that are natural to him. I grew up hungry and lonely, a witness to human suffering and injustice; my mind is filled with sympathy for humanity in general and outrage over a society that bristles with inequality. That's what my stories are all about, that's all they *could* be about. Not surprisingly, as my stomach grew accustomed to being full when I wanted it to be, my literary output underwent a change. I have gradually come to realize that a life of eating *jiaozi* three times a day can still be accompanied by pain and suffering, and that this spiritual suffering is no less painful than physical hunger. The act of giving voice to this spiritual suffering is, in my view, the sacred duty of a writer. But for me, writing about the suffering of the soul in no way supplants my concern for the physical agony brought about by hunger. I can't say whether this is my strength as a writer, or my weakness, but I know it is what fate has decreed for me.

My earliest writing is probably better left unmentioned. But mention it I must, since it is part and parcel of my life story and of China's recent literary history. I still recall my very first story. In it I wrote about the digging of a canal. A junior militia officer begins the morning by standing before a portrait of our Chairman Mao and offering up a simple prayer: May You Live Ten Thousand Years, May You Live Ten Thousand Years, May You Live Ten Thousand Years! He then leaves to attend a meeting in the village, where it is decided that he will take his production team to a spot beyond the village and dig a gigantic canal. To show her support for this enterprise, his fiancée decides to postpone their marriage for three years. When a local landlord hears of the planned excavation, he sneaks into the production team's livestock area in the dead of night, picks up a shovel, and smashes the leg of a black mule scheduled to pull a cart at the canal work site. Class struggle.

Reacting as if the enemy were at hand, the people mobilize themselves for a violent struggle against the class enemy. Eventually, the canal is dug and the landlord seized. No one these days would deign to read such a story, but that was just about all anyone wrote back then. It was the only way you could get published. So that's what I wrote. And still I wasn't able to see it into print — not revolutionary enough.

As the 1970s wound down, our Chairman Mao died, and the situation in China began to change, including its literary output. But the changes were both feeble and slow. Forbidden topics ran the gamut from love stories to tales of Party blunders; but the yearning for freedom was not to be denied. Writers racked their brains to find ways, however roundabout, to break the taboos. This period saw the rise of so-called scar literature, personal accounts of the horrors of the Cultural Revolution. My own career didn't really start until the early 1980s, when Chinese literature had already undergone significant changes. Few forbidden topics remained, and many Western writers were introduced into the country, creating a frenzy of Chinese imitations.

As a child who grew up in a grassy field, enjoying little formal education, I know virtually nothing about literary theories and have had to rely solely upon my own experiences and intuitive understanding of the world to write. Literary fads that all but monopolized literary circles, including recasting the works of foreign writers in Chinese, were not for me. I knew I had to write what was natural to me, something clearly different from what other writers, Western and Chinese, were writing. This does not mean that Western writing exerted no influence on me. Quite the contrary: I have been profoundly influenced by some Western writers, and am happy to openly acknowledge that influence. But what sets me apart from other Chinese writers is that I neither copy the narrative techniques of foreign writers nor imitate their story lines; what I am happy to do is closely explore what is embedded in their work in order to understand their observations of life and comprehend how they view the world we live in. In my mind, by reading the works of others, a writer is actually engaging in a dialogue, maybe even a romance in which, if there is a meeting of the minds, a lifelong friendship is born; if not, an amicable parting is fine, too.

Up to this point, three of my novels have been published in America: *Red Sorghum*, *The Garlic Ballads*, and *The Republic of Wine*. *Red Sorghum* exposes the reader to my understanding of history and of love. In *The Garlic Ballads* I reveal a critical view of politics and my sympathy for China's peasants. *The Republic of Wine* expresses my sorrow over the decline of humanity and my loathing of a corrupt bureaucracy. On the surface, each of these novels appears to be radically different from the others, but at their core they are very much alike; they all express a yearning for the good life by a lonely child afraid of going hungry.

The same is true of my shorter works. In China, the short story has little standing. In the eyes of writers and critics alike, only novelists count as worthy creators of fiction, while writers of shorter fiction are practitioners of a petty craft. Forgive me when I say that this is wrong-headed. The stature of a writer can only be determined by the thought revealed in a work, not by its length. A writer's place in a nation's literary history cannot be judged by whether or not he is capable of writing a book as heavy as a brick. That must rest on his contributions to the development and enrichment of that nation's language.

I venture to say, immodest though it may seem, that my novels have created a unique style of writing in contemporary Chinese literature. Yet I take even greater pride in what I've been able to accomplish in the realm of short stories. Over the past fifteen years or so, I have published some eighty stories, eight of which are included in this collection, selected by my translator, with my wholehearted approval. They represent both the range of themes and variety of styles of my short story output over the years. Once you have finished this volume, you will have a good picture of what I've tried to do in my shorter fiction.

"Shifu, You'll Do Anything for a Laugh" is my latest story (it has recently been filmed by China's preëminent director, Zhang Yimou, under the title *Happy Days*). While at first it may appear to deal primarily with the "downsizing" problem facing today's Chinese workers, in line with the Chinese saying, "Alcoholism is not really about alcohol," there is more to the story than meets the eye. What I also want to show is how young couples in love are forced to sneak around to share their love. "Abandoned Child," written in the mid-1980s, concerns one of contemporary Chinese society's thorniest problems — enforced family planning in a pervasive climate of valuing boys over girls. Decades of governmental efforts in implementing a one-child policy have produced impressive results in China's urban centers, where the long-held concept of "boys are better than girls" has undergone a change. But in the countryside, families with more than one child are still the norm, and the general disdain for baby girls is as prevalent as ever. Unchecked population growth remains China's most serious predicament, and a host of social problems emanating from the one-child policy are already beginning to appear.

"Man and Beast," also written in the 1980s, continues the family saga of *Red Sorghum* and describes how, under extraordinary circumstances, the last shreds of humanity can give rise to a blaze of glory. Toward the end of the 1980s I wrote "Love Story," a tale of puppy love. Set in the ten years of the disastrous Cultural Revolution, when hundreds of thousands of young men and women were sent from the cities up to the mountains and down to the countryside, the story tells of a young country boy who falls in love with a city girl much older than he, an uncommon turn of events. But it is precisely this feature that allows me to explore the concepts of sadness and beauty.

"The Cure," "Iron Child," and "Soaring" are all part of a series of short pieces I wrote during the early 1990s. "The Cure" is a tale of cannibalism and cruelty, and "Iron Child" and "Soaring" can be read as fables. Finally, there is "Shen Garden," one of my last stories of the twentieth century. What I want to show here is how a middle-aged man turns his back on the love of an earlier time and eventually compromises with reality. In today's society, many Chinese men who have achieved success, even fame, live hypocritical lives. Deep down, their existence is little more than a pile of ruins.

As I have said, I am a writer with no theoretical training; but I possess a fertile imagination, thanks in part to China's popular traditions, which I am intent on continuing. I may be ignorant of high-flown literary concepts, but I do know how to spin a bewitching tale, something I learned as a child from my grandfather, my grandmother, and a variety of village story-tellers. Critics who base their views of literature on scientific theories of one sort or another don't think much of me. But let's see them write a story that captures a reader's imagination.

M.Y.
Beijing, 2001

Translator's Note

The term *shifu* is a generic and generally respectful term for skilled workers and the like; widely used, it has, in a sense, replaced other terms, such as "comrade." It is common in China to use kinship or professional forms of address in preference to given names.

The Shen Garden in the story of that title, which was located in the southern city of Shaoxing over a millennium ago, is famous as a metaphor for encounters between once married couples. It is where the Southern Song poet Lu You is said to have met Tang Wan, whom his parents had forced him to divorce.

"The Cure" (literally, "effective medicine") is an updated version of the famous story "Medicine" by Lu Xun (1881–1936), twentieth-century China's most renowned literary figure. In the earlier story, a child is treated for consumption with the blood of a beheaded revolutionary, but dies nonetheless; it too is a caustic satire on contemporary society and politics.

The translator thanks the editor of the Hong Kong magazine *Renditions* for her editorial suggestions on the story

"Soaring" and for permission to reprint. "The Cure" appeared in slightly modified form in my anthology *Chairman Mao Would Not Be Amused* (Grove Press, 1995). As always, my thanks to Li-chun for checking the manuscript and to Mo Yan for his generosity and cooperation. Both have made the translator's job especially rewarding and enjoyable.

SHIFU, YOU'LL DO ANYTHING FOR A LAUGH

Shifu, You'll Do Anything for a Laugh

1

DING SHIKOU, OR TEN MOUTH DING, HAD WORKED AT THE Municipal Farm Equipment Factory for forty-three years and was a month away from mandatory retirement age when he was abruptly laid off. Now if you put shi (十), the word for *ten*, inside a kou (口), the word for *mouth*, you get the word tian (田), for *field*. The family name Ding can mean a strapping young man. As long as a strapping young man has a field to tend, he'll never have to worry about having food on the table and clothes on his back. That was his farmer father's cherished wish for his son when he named him. But Ding Shikou was not destined to own land; instead he found work in a factory, which led to a far better life than he'd have had as a farmer. He was enormously grateful to the society that had brought him so much happiness, and was determined to pay it back through hard work. Decades of exhausting labor had bent him over, and even though he wasn't yet sixty, he had the look of a man in his seventies.

One morning, like all other workday mornings, he rode to the factory on his 1960s black and obstinate, clunky Grand Defense bicycle, which presented quite a sight among all the sleek lightweight bikes on the street. Young cyclists, male and female, first gave him curious stares, then steered clear of him, the way a fancy sedan gets out of the way of a lumbering tank. As soon as he pedaled through the factory gate, he saw a group of people clustered around the bulletin board. The voices of a couple of women rose above the general buzz, like hens about to lay eggs. His heart fluttered as he realized that what the workers feared most had finally happened.

He parked his bike and took a look around, exchanging a meaningful glance with old Qin Tou, the gateman. Then, with a heavy sigh, he slowly walked over to join the crowd. His heart was heavy, but not too heavy. After word of imminent layoffs at the factory had gotten out, he went to see the factory manager, a refined middle-aged man, who graciously invited him to sit on the light-green lambskin sofa. Then he asked his secretary to bring them tea. As Ding held the glass of scalding liquid and smelled its jasmine fragrance, he was engulfed in gratitude, and suddenly found himself tongue-tied. After smoothing out his high-quality suit and sitting up straight on the opposite sofa, the factory manager said with a little laugh:

"Ding Shifu, I know why you're here. After several years of financial setbacks here at the factory, layoffs have become un-avoidable. But you're a veteran worker, a provincial model worker, a *shifu* — master worker — and even if we're down to the last man, that man will be you."

People were crowding up to the bulletin board, and from his vantage point behind them, Ding Shikou caught a glimpse of three large sheets of paper filled with writing. Over the past few decades, his name had appeared on that bulletin board several times a year, and always on red paper; those were the times he had been honored as an advanced or model worker. He tried to elbow his way up front, but was jostled so badly by the youngsters that he wound up moving backward. Amid all the curses and grumbling, a woman burst out crying. He knew at once it was Wang Dalan, the warehouse storekeeper. She'd started out as a punch-press operator, but had mangled one of her hands in an accident, and when gangrene set in they'd had to amputate it to save her life. Since it was a job-related injury, the factory kept her on as a storekeeper.

Just then a white Jeep Cherokee drove in the gate honking its horn, seizing the attention of the people fighting to read the layoff list; they all turned to stare at the Jeep, which looked as if it had just come back from a long, muddy trip. The clamor died down as dazed expressions showed on the people's faces. The Jeep looked a little dazed too, its horn suddenly silent, the engine sputtering, the tailpipe spitting out puffs of exhaust. It was like a wild beast that sensed danger. Its gray eyes stared as they fearfully sized up the situation. At roughly the same time it decided to back out through the gate a chorus of shouts erupted from the workers, whose legs got the message, and in no time the Jeep was surrounded. It tried to break free, lurching forward and backward a time or two, but it was too late. A tall, muscular young man with a purple face — Ding Shikou saw that it was his apprentice, Lü Xiaohu — bent down, opened the car door, and jerked the assistant manager in charge of supply and marketing right out of his seat. Curses rained down on the man's head, translucent gobs of spittle splattered on his face, which by then was a ghostly white. His greasy hair fell down over his eyes as he clasped his hands in front of his chest, bent low at the waist, and bowed, first to Lü Xiaohu, then to the rest of the crowd. His lips were moving, but whatever he was trying to say was drowned out by the threatening noises around him. Ding couldn't make out a single word, but there was no mistaking the wretched look on the man's face, like a thief who'd been caught in the act. The next thing he saw was Lü Xiaohu reach out to grab the assistant manager's colorful necktie, which looked like a newly-weds' quilt, and jerk it straight down; the assistant manager disappeared from view, as if he'd fallen down a well.

A pair of police cars stormed up to the compound, sirens blaring. This threw such a scare into Ding Shikou, whose heart was racing, that all he could think of was getting the hell out of there; too bad he couldn't get his legs to follow orders. Finding it impossible to drive through the gate, the police parked their cars outside the compound and poured out of the cars; there were seven of them in all — four fat ones and three skinny ones. Armed with batons, handcuffs, walkie-talkies, pistols, bullets, tear gas, and a battery-powered bullhorn, the seven cops took a few unhurried steps, then stopped just outside the gate to form a cordon, as if to seal off the factory gate as an escape route. A closer look showed that they probably weren't going to seal off the factory, after all. One of the cops, who was getting along in years, raised the bullhorn to his mouth and ordered the workers to disperse, which they did. Like a wolf exposed in the field when sorghum stalks are cut down, the assistant manager for supply and marketing popped into view. He was sprawled on the ground, facedown, protecting his head with his hands, his rear end sticking up in the air, looking like a frightened ostrich. The cop handed his bullhorn to the man beside him and walked up to the cowering assistant manager; he reached down and took hold of the man's collar with his thumb and two fingers, as if to lift him to his feet, but the assistant manager looked as though he was trying to dig a hole for himself. His suit coat separated itself from him, forming a little tent. Now Ding could hear what he was shouting:

"Don't blame me, good people. I've just returned from Hainan Island, and I don't know a thing. You can't blame me for this. . . ."

Without letting go of the man's coat, the policeman nudged his leg with the tip of his shoe. "Get up," he said, "right now!"

The assistant manager got to his feet, and when he saw that the person he'd gotten up for was a policeman, his phlegm-splattered face suddenly became the color of a dirt roadway. His legs buckled, and the only reason he didn't crumple to the ground again was that the policeman was still holding him by the collar.

Before long, the factory manager drove up in his red VW Santana, followed by the vice mayor for industry in a black Audi. The factory manager was sweating, his eyes tear-filled; after bowing deeply three times to the workers, he confessed to them that he was powerless in an unfeeling market that was taking a factory with a glorious history down the road to financial disaster, and that if they kept losing money, they'd have to close up shop. He wrapped up his tale of woe by calling attention to old Ding. After recapping old Ding's glorious career, he told them he had no choice but to lay him off, even though old Ding was scheduled to retire in a month.

Like a man who has been awakened from a dream, old Ding turned to look at the red sheets of paper tacked up on the bulletin board. There, right at the top of the lay-off list, in alphabetical order, he spotted his own name. He circled his fellow workers, with the look of a child searchng for his mother; but all he saw was a sea of identical dull gray faces. Suddenly light-headed, he squatted down on his haunches; when that proved too tiring, he sat down on the ground. He hadn't been sitting there long before he burst into tears. His loud wails were far more infectious than those of the females in the crowd, and as his fellow workers' faces darkened, they too began to cry. Through tear-clouded eyes he watched Vice Mayor Ma, that agreeable, friendly man, walk toward him in the company of the factory manager. Flustered by the sight, he stopped crying, propped himself up by his hands, and got shakily to his feet. The vice mayor reached out and shook his grimy hand. Old Ding marveled over the softness of the man's hand, like dough, not a bone anywhere. When he thrust out his other hand, the vice mayor reached out with his free hand to take it. Four hands were tightly clasped as he heard the vice mayor say:

"Comrade Ding, I thank you on behalf of the municipal government and Party Committee."

Ding's nose began to ache and the tears gushed again.

"Come see me anytime," the vice mayor said.

2

Originally, the Municipal Farm Equipment Factory had been a capitalist operation called Prosperity Metalworks, which

6

produced mainly kitchen cleavers and scythes. After it became a semipublic company, its name was changed to the Red Star Metalworks. It produced the Red Star two-wheeled, double-shared plow, which had been so popular in the 1950s; then in the 1960s it specialized in the Red Star cotton seeder. In the 1970s its name was changed to the Farm Equipment Manufacturing and Repair Company, producing millet and corn threshers. In the 1980s, it manufactured sprinklers and small reapers. In the 1990s, using new equipment imported from Germany, it produced pull-tab beverage cans; its name was changed once again, this time to Silesia Farm Machinery Group, but people habitually referred to it as Farm Equipment Manufacturing and Repair.

After shaking hands so warmly with Vice Mayor Ma, Ding was caught up in a mood of empty joy, the sort of feeling he'd had as a young man after climbing off his wife. His restless, seething fellow workers began to calm down in the presence of the police, the vice mayor, and the factory manager. Without intending to, old Ding set a fine example for all the workers. He heard the factory manager say to the assembled workers: "Who among you can boast of old Ding's seniority? Or match his contributions? Just look at how quietly he's taking the news. So why are the rest of you kicking up such a row?" Then it was the vice mayor's turn: "Comrades, you can learn a lesson from Ding Shifu by looking at the big picture and not making things hard on the government. We will do everything in our power to create new job opportunities, so you won't be out of work for long. But between now and then, you'll have to come up with something on your own and not just rely on the government." With mounting excitement, he added, "Comrades, if members of the working class can reverse the course of events with their own two hands, it shouldn't be hard to find a way to make a living, should it?"

The vice mayor drove off in his black Audi, followed by the factory manager in his red Santana. Even the now disheveled assistant factory manager drove off in his white Cherokee. The crowd of workers grumbled a while longer before breaking up and heading home. Lü Xiaohu walked up and took a leak on the bulletin board, then turned and said to old Ding, who was propped up against a tree:

"Let's go, Shifu. You'll go hungry hanging around here. The old man's dead and the old lady's remarried, so it's every man for himself."

Old Ding nodded to Qin Tou, the gateman, and walked his Grand Defense bicycle through the factory gate. Qin Tou called out to him, "Wait up, Ding Shifu!"

He stopped just beyond the gate and watched the former high school teacher come running up to him. Everyone knew that old Qin was well connected, which was how he was able to take on the light duties of a gateman and newspaper delivery-man after retiring as a schoolteacher. When he caught up to old Ding, he reached into his pocket and took out a business card.

"Ding Shifu," he said somberly, "my second son-in-law is a reporter for the provincial newspaper. This is his card. Go ask him to plead your case in the court of public opinion."

Old Ding hesitated a moment before taking the card. Then he swung his unwilling leg over his Grand Defense and started off. But he hadn't ridden more than a couple of feet before his legs began to ache badly; he lurched sideways and fell off, the heavy bicycle crashing down and pinning him to the ground. Old Qin ran up, lifted the bicycle off, and helped him to his feet.

"Are you okay, Ding Shifu?" old Qin asked with genuine concern.

Once again he thanked old Qin and headed home slowly, walking his bike this time. Warm April breezes brushing against his face infused feelings of emptiness, sort of saccharine sweet. He felt dizzy, borderline drunk. Clusters of snowy poplar blossoms on the road by the curbs waved back and forth. A flock of homing pigeons circled in the sky above him, their trainers' whistles falling on his ears. He was a long way from crushing torment, yet he couldn't stop the river of tears running down his cheeks. As he passed a neighborhood park near his house, a little boy chasing a ball ran smack into him, sending shooting pains up his leg that forced him to sit down beside the road. The little boy looked up at him.

"Gramps," he said, "how come you're crying?"

He wiped his eyes with his sleeve and said, "You're a nice little boy. I'm not crying. Got some sand in my eyes. . . ."

3

His leg ached terribly when he got home, so he asked his wife to go out and buy a couple of medicinal patches. But these actually made the pain worse, and now he had no choice but to go see a doctor. Since they were childless, his wife asked Lü Xiaohu to take him to the hospital on his three-wheel cart. An X ray showed he had a fracture.

Two months later, he hobbled out of the hospital with the

help of a cane. The two-month hospital stay and all the medication had nearly wiped out the old couple's savings. Armed
with his cane and a pipe dream, he went to the factory with a
fistful of receipts and a head full of illusions. But the gate was
closed and locked and the compound was still as death. For the
first time, he felt truly wronged. Banging his cane on the metal
gate, he shouted at the top of his lungs. The gate emitted a
hollow sound, like the late-night barks of a dog. Finally, old
Qin stuck his head out of the gatehouse and asked through the
gate, "Is that you, Ding Shifu?"

"Where's the factory manager? I need to see him."

Old Qin shook his head and smiled wryly, not saying a word.

Lü Xiaohu, who had come along with him, had an idea:
"Here's what I think, Shifu. Go over and sit in front of the government offices. Either that or set yourself on fire."

"What did you say?"

"I'm not saying you should set yourself on fire," Lü Xiaohu
said with a smile. "Just give them a scare. They care about face
more than anything."

"What kind of idea is that?" Ding said. "Are you asking me
to go put on an act?"

"What else can you do? Shifu, a man your age can't keep up
with the rest of us. We've got our youth and our strength, so we
can still make a living. But the government's all you've got
left."

Ding neither sat in nor burned himself up, but he did
hobble up to the government office gate, where he was
stopped by a gateman in a blue tunic.

"I'm here to see Vice Mayor Ma," he said, "Vice Mayor
Ma . . ."

The gateman gave him a cold, hard look, without saying a word. But the minute he tried to walk through the gate, the gateman grabbed him and jerked him back. "I said I'm here to see Vice Mayor Ma," he shouted as he struggled to break free. "He told me to come see him."

His patience quickly exhausted, the gateman shoved him backward; Ding stumbled a few steps before plopping down on the ground. He could have gotten back up, but he just sat there, feeling miserable and wanting to cry. So he did. At first it was just some silent sobs, but before long, he was really bawling. Rubberneckers began drifting over to see what was wrong. No one said a word. Embarrassed by the gathering crowd, he knew he should get up and leave, but just walking away would be even more embarrassing. So he shut his eyes and really cut loose. Then he heard Lü Xiaohu's shrill voice rise from the crowd. After relating Ding's glorious past to the crowd, Lü started to complain about his treatment, trying to stir up the crowd. Ding felt something hard hit him on the leg. When he opened his eyes, he saw a one-yuan coin flopping around in the mud next to his leg. Then more coins and bills fell all around him.

A squad of policemen came running up out of nowhere, their rhythmic footsteps sounding like the jackhammers made by the Farm Equipment Manufacturing and Repair Factory. Waving their batons, the police tried to disperse the crowd, but the people wouldn't budge. That led to pushing and shoving, and as Ding watched legs fly around him and heard the shouts and shrieks, he was overcome with guilt feelings. No matter what, he couldn't keep sitting there.

As he was getting to his feet, three well-dressed men rushed out of the government office building, two refined-looking young men in front, a fair-skinned, fleshy, middle-aged man bringing up the rear. They seemed almost buoyant, as if carried along by the wind. When they reached the gate, the two young men stepped aside to let their middle-aged companion walk ahead. Their movements were practiced and orderly; they were well trained. With a wave of the man's hand and a crisp order, the police backed off; the scene was reminiscent of a father breaking up a fight between his son and a neighbor boy by pulling a long face and telling his son to get the hell out of there. That done, he assumed a gentler tone in asking the crowd to disperse. Lü Xiaohu elbowed his way up front and spoke to the middle-aged man, who bent toward old Ding and said:

"Good uncle, Vice Mayor Ma is at a meeting in the provincial capital. My name is Wu, I'm Assistant Director of the General Office. Tell me what it is you want."

Ding choked up as he gazed into the kindly face of Assistant Director Wu.

"Good uncle," Assistant Director Wu said, "come into my office. We can talk there."

With a sign from Assistant Director Wu, the two young men walked up and took old Ding by the arms to walk him into the building, followed by Assistant Director Wu, who was carrying his cane.

As he sat in the air-conditioned office sipping hot water that Assistant Director Wu had personally poured for him, the blockage in his throat went away, and he talked about his suffering and his troubles. Once he'd stated his case, he took out the bundle of expenditure receipts. Assistant Director Wu responded with an explanation of how things stood, then took a hundred-yuan bill out of his pocket and said:

"Ding Shifu, you hold on to those receipts. When Vice Mayor Ma returns, I'll give him a complete report on your situation. But for now, I'd like you to have this hundred yuan."

Old Ding stood up with the help of his cane and said:

"You're a good man, Assistant Director Wu, and I thank you." He bowed to the man. "But I can't accept your money."

4

In the days that followed, he ignored his apprentice's advice to return to the government building to put on his act again, even though no one showed up from Vice Mayor Ma's office. His wife complained that his pride was making their lives a living hell, and scolded him by saying you can't help a dead cat climb a tree. He reacted by smashing a teacup and glaring venomously into his wife's gaunt, ashen face. The courage to stand up to him lasted only a moment. Then, lowering her head and reaching into her apron pocket to take out her badly worn black Naugahyde wallet, she put the responsibility squarely on his shoulders: "We have exactly ninety-nine yuan. When that's gone, there's no more."

She turned on her heel and went into the kitchen, from where chopping sounds soon emerged. Preparing soup bones. A moment later, she returned. Nestled in her hand, which was covered with bone splinters, was a one-yuan coin. "My apologies," she said gravely. "Here's another yuan. I was using it to prop up the table leg. I nearly forgot about it."

A strange smile appeared on her face as she laid the coin down beside her wallet. He glowered at her, wanting her to look at him. All he needed was for their eyes to meet for him to have the chance to silently unload half a lifetime of discontent toward her. Because she was infertile, in his eyes she was simply inferior. But she shrewdly turned around, taking the brunt of his rage on her back. She was wearing a black synthetic blouse with yellow flowers, something she'd picked up somewhere or other and which was utterly inappropriate for a woman her age. A sunflower the size of a basin cast an aging ray onto her slightly hunched back. Raising his fist, with the idea of pounding the hell out of the wallet on the table, he stopped in midair, sighed despondently, and sat down, defeated. Any man who can't make a living and take care of his family has no right to lash out at his wife. That's the way it's always been, in China and in other places.

One sunny morning, he put away his cane and walked out the door. With the sun's blinding rays stinging his eyes, he felt a bit like a mole that's come out into the light after years in a dark hole. A rainbow array of automobiles passed slowly in front of him, with motorcycles shuttling in and out among them, like defiant jackrabbits. He wanted to cross the street, but didn't have the nerve to weave his way through the stream of cars. A vague memory of an overpass somewhere nearby surfaced, so he started walking down the sidewalk, with its newly laid, colorful cement tiles. He may have lived in the city for many years, but he discovered that he wasn't even as brave as a common villager he spotted riding an unwieldy bicycle down the street. The man was carrying a gas can with sweet potatoes baking inside; with steam pouring off the back of his bike, even fancy sedans gave way to him. A pair of villagers with saws and axes over their shoulders strolled down the street, whistling; the shorter of the two, wearing a corduroy jacket, carefree as can be, swung his ax at the trunk of an Oriental plane tree. Old Ding shuddered, almost as if he had been the target of the chopping blow. Peddlers' stands filled the tree-lined street, one every few paces, and nearly every one of them hailed him as he passed by. They displayed a motley array of wares, as large as electric appliances and as small as buttons, and everything in between. One of them, a dark-skinned man with slanted eyes, was squatting beneath a tree, a cigarette dangling from his lips and a pair of fat little piglets on tethers.

"Old uncle, how about a nice piglet?" the peddler asked fervently. "They're real Yorkshires, the finest breed you can find. They make great pets, clean and neat, much better than dogs or cats. In the West they're more popular than dogs and cats. A United Nations study has proved that the only animals smarter than pigs are people. Pigs can recognize words, they can paint pictures, and if you've got the patience, you can even teach them to sing and dance." He took a crumpled newspaper clipping out of his pocket, stuck the tethers under his foot to free both hands, and pointed to the clipping. "Old uncle," he said, "you don't have to believe me, it's right here in black and white. See here — an elderly Irish woman raised a pig, and it was the same as hiring a nanny. Every morning, after bringing in the paper, it went out and bought her some milk and bread. Then it scrubbed the floor and boiled water, but most amazing of all, one day the old woman had a heart attack, and that smart little pig went straight to the local clinic for an ambulance. It saved that old woman's life. . . ."

Thanks to the peddler's honeyed words, the sort of good mood he hadn't enjoyed for a very long time settled upon Ding. He cast a warm, tender gaze down at the piglets, which were tethered by their rear legs and huddled closely together, like a pair of inseparable twins. Their bristles glistened like silver threads, their bellies sported black spots. Their snouts were pink, their little eyes like shiny black marbles. A pudgy little girl with pigtails that stuck straight up waddled up and squatted in front of the piglets, entering old Ding's field of vision. Frightened by the little girl, the piglets pulled in opposite directions, squealing like a couple of puppies. Next to enter his field of vision was a young woman with a radiant face who reached out both arms — her skin milky white — and scooped up the little girl, who kicked and howled so much that the woman had to put her back down on the ground. Showing no fear at all, the little girl went right up next to the piglets, which squeezed up against each other. She reached out with her dainty little hand, and the piglets squeezed together even tighter and began to quake. Finally, she touched one of them. It squealed, but didn't try to get away. Looking up at the young woman, the girl giggled. The peddler saw it was time to put his three-inch weapon of a tongue into play. He repeated his earlier sales pitch, this time spicing it up even more. The woman kept her eyes on him, a captivating smile frozen on her lips. She was wearing an orange-colored dress, bright as a flaming torch and so low-cut that when she bent over, her full breasts crept into view. Old Ding couldn't help glancing over at her, much to his embarrassment, as if he'd done something he really shouldn't have done. He noticed that the pig seller had his eyes glued on the exact same spot. Every time the woman tried to pick up the little girl, her plan was shattered by the little girl's tantrum. Old Ding noticed a heavy gold necklace around the woman's neck and deep green jade bracelets on both arms. And he couldn't miss the woman's heavy fragrance: sweeter smelling than the jasmine tea he'd been given in the factory reception room, sweeter smelling than the perfume the factory secretary wore, so sweet smelling it made him giddy. Knowing instinctively where his sale was coming from, the peddler zeroed in on the little girl, regaling her with all the advantages of raising pigs and holding his little piglets right up in front of her, despite their noisy struggles to keep a distance between them and her. Scratching one pig's belly, then the other's, he said to the little girl in the sweetest tone of voice he could manage, "Go ahead, little sister, touch the two little cuties."

Now that they'd been scratched, the piglets calmed down and grunted contentedly, gazing off into the distance as they rocked back and forth a bit before settling softly onto the ground. The little girl summoned up the courage to tug one of their ears and gently poke its belly. More contented grunts as both the little pigs started to fall asleep.

Having made up her mind to leave, the woman picked up the little girl, only to spark yet another tantrum. She put her down again, and as soon as the little feet hit the ground, they headed unsteadily right for the piglets; no more tears. A crafty smile spread across the peddler's face as he launched into yet another sales pitch.

"How much for one of those?" the woman asked him.

After a thoughtful "hmm," he replied decisively:

"For anybody else, three hundred apiece, but you can have the pair for five hundred."

"Can't you make it a little less?" she asked.

"Young lady, take a good look at those pigs. You don't see animals like that every day. They're purebred, living, breathing Yorkshires! Go to the toy section of any department store, and you'll find that a toy pig will cost you a couple of hundred! If my son weren't getting married and didn't need money to set up a household, I wouldn't part with these two for five thousand yuan, let alone five hundred!"

The woman smiled sweetly. "Slow down," she said. "The next thing you'll be telling me is that they're a pair of unicorns!"

"That's not far from the truth!"

"I didn't bring any money with me."

"No problem. I'll deliver them to your door."

But when the peddler tugged on the tethers to leave, the piglets started scurrying back and forth, and he was forced to pick them up and tuck one under each arm. They squealed their displeasure.

"Stop squealing, little ones. Luck is with us today. You're about to become the happiest little pigs in the world. Joyful days are here for you two. Instead of squealing like that, you should be laughing."

The peddler followed the woman into a lane, a pig under each arm. The little girl, who was perched on the woman's shoulders, turned around and laughed loudly at the sight of the pigs.

Old Ding watched the procession of pigs and people as long as he could with a growing sense of melancholy. Then he started walking again, all the way up to the middle of the overpass, where he stopped and thought dreamily about the captivating elegance of the young woman. The bridge too was crowded with little stalls, each one manned by a peddler who had the look of a laid-off worker. The overpass swayed slightly; gusts of hot wind hit him in the face. Cars whizzed back and forth on the sparkling asphalt below. He spotted his apprentice, Lü Xiaohu, wearing a yellow vest, speeding down the sidewalk across the way on his three-wheeled pedicab. A white canopy over the back shielded a stately young couple. They were traveling so fast he couldn't see the spokes in the wheels, which were just a silvery blur. The two heads behind the man up front touched from time to time. Sweat poured down Lü Xiaohu's face. He was no one to mess with, old Ding was thinking, but was a terrific fitter, and any fitter worthy of the name was good at just about anything he put his hand to.

After walking down off the overpass, he entered a farmer's market, filled with hope. The canopy over the market was made of green nylon, which gave the faces of all the vegetable sellers a green tint. The smell of vegetables, meat, fish, and fried snacks merged and engulfed him; so did the shouts of hawking peddlers. In front of one of the stalls he spotted Wang Dalan, the one-handed woman who had worked with him at the factory. She was watching over a pile of sticky strawberries.

"Ding Shifu," she called to him warmly. "Where have you been keeping yourself?"

He stopped in his tracks. And when he did, he spotted three more former workers from the factory. They all smiled at him. Then they asked him to sample their wares.

"Have some strawberries, Ding Shifu!"

"How about a tomato, Ding Shifu?"

"Try one of my carrots, Ding Shifu!"

He was about to ask them how business was, until he got a good look at their faces. There was no need to ask. Life was tough, all right, but as long as you were willing to work hard and put your pride aside, you could always get by. But there was no way a man his age could compete with younger folks in opening a vegetable stall, let alone pedaling a pedicab like his apprentice. He also couldn't sell piglets out on the street; you couldn't call it hard work, but you needed the gift of gab, someone who could talk a dead man into coming back to life. At the factory, old Ding had a reputation for almost never having anything to say. This was all very disappointing, but he hadn't reached the point of despair. He'd take a look around and find something he could do. In fact, that's what he was doing now. He refused to believe that in a city this big, there wasn't a single thing he could do to make a living. And just as despair was beginning to creep in, the old man upstairs pointed out the way to riches.

Dusk was falling when he found himself in front of the hill behind the factory, where the blood-red rays of the setting sun danced on the brilliant surface of the man-made pond behind the hill. Carefree couples strolled along the path ringing the lake. After decades of working at the factory, this was the first time he'd ever made his way out to the hill, let alone strolled around the lake. For all those years, the factory had been his second home; the dozens of awards he'd earned represented buckets of sweat. He turned back to look once more at the factory: a workshop that had once buzzed with activity now stood quiet and deserted. The clang of steel on steel had become yesterday's dream; the chimney that had spewed black smoke for decades was now a sleeping volcano; the factory grounds were littered with tin can rejects and rusty cutting machinery; the yard behind the cafeteria was strewn with empty liquor bottles.

The factory was dead; a factory with no workers was nothing less than a graveyard. His eyes burned, his heart was filled with a mixture of sadness and anger. As the evening deepened, an eerie gloom rose above the hilltop thickets, heralded by the shriek of a bird that startled him. He massaged his sore leg and stood up. He walked back down the hill.

A cemetery occupied the area near the lake at the foot of the hill. It was the final resting place of over a hundred heroes from the life-and-death struggles of the city thirty years before. Lush green trees ringed the cemetery: there were pines, cypresses, and dozens of towering poplars. He walked over to the cemetery on a leg so sore he had to sit down on a stone marker. Crows saturated the night with caws from a nest in one of the poplars and magpies circled above as he massaged his leg. While he was rubbing it, his gaze drifted to the abandoned hulk of a bus on the ground beneath the poplar. No tires, no glass in the windows, and hardly any paint anywhere. Who, he wondered, left that thing here? And why? Occupational habit had him thinking how he could convert the thing into a living space. And at that moment he spotted a young couple skulking out of the cemetery, like a pair of specters, then slipping into the rusty bus. For some strange reason, he began breathing hard. One old Ding wanted only to get out of there as quickly as possible; a second old Ding couldn't tear himself away. While the two old Dings were engaged in a fierce battle of wills, a soft, lovely moan emerged from the bus hulk. That was followed by an irrepressible female scream, not all that different from the screech of a cat in heat, but distinct nonetheless. Old Ding couldn't see his own face, of course, but his ears were burning and even the puffs of air from his nose seemed overheated. There was a rustling noise in the bus just before the man popped out through the door. The woman followed a few moments later. He held his breath like a thief hiding in the bushes, not getting slowly to his feet until he heard a somewhat triumphant cough coming from the line of trees beyond the cemetery.

The old Ding who wanted to leave and the more curious old Ding engaged in yet another battle of wills; on and on they fought as his legs carried him into the bus. The dark, murky interior was damp and musty smelling. Gray litter was scattered around the floor; he nudged some of it with the tip of his shoe and decided it was toilet paper.

A husky voice called to him from outside:

"Shifu — Ding Shifu — where are you?"

It was his apprentice, Lü Xiaohu.

He walked outside and took a few cautious steps forward to calm himself before replying:

"Stop shouting, I'm in here!"

5

Lü Xiaohu was pedaling so hard he could barely talk:

"Your wife was worried half to death, said you had a funny look in your eyes when you left the house, afraid you might do something foolish, try to end it all. I told her you'd never do anything like that, not somebody as smart as you. I told her I knew where you'd be, and I was right. Shifu, screw the factory, now that it's turned into this. If an earthworm in the ground won't starve to death, then neither will we, the working class."

He was watching his apprentice's back lurch from side to side from his seat in the pedicab and listening to him prattle, and while his heart was awash with feelings, he didn't make a sound. It felt to him as if a hot current were racing through his body, and in that moment, the gloom that had accompanied him ever since getting laid off simply vanished. His heart was like the sky after a rainfall. The pedicab turned into a busy street, where the flashing neon lights gave him an incomparable rush. Barbecue stalls lined the street, filling his nose with aromatic smoke. Suddenly a shout: Environmental cops! The peddlers jumped on their bicycles and pedaled off with their smoky barbecue stalls behind them, straight into the maze of neighborhood lanes. Their dispersal went off like clockwork, like a perfectly executed drill, no straggling, like a school of fish diving en masse to the bottom of a river, leaving not a trace.

"Did you see that, Shifu?" his apprentice asked. "Chickens follow their ways and dogs follow theirs. After getting laid off, everyone comes up with his own brilliant idea."

s they were passing a public toilet, old Ding reached out and tapped his apprentice on the shoulder. "Stop," he said.

He walked up to the toilet, a building made of white ceramic tiles with a green glazed tile roof. A young fellow sitting in a glass booth rapped the glass with his finger, calling his attention to the red lettering on the window:

PAY TOILET   ONE YUAN PER VISIT

He put his hand in his pocket. Empty, not a cent. Lü Xiaohu walked up and pushed two yuan through the crescent opening in the booth. "Come in with me, Shifu," he said.

A sense of shame welled up in old Ding's heart, not because he had no money, but because he hadn't known that he had to pay to use the toilet. After following his apprentice inside the brightly lit toilet, his nostrils were assailed by a strangely sweet reek that made his head swim. The floor tiles were so glossy he could see his reflection in them, and he faltered, nearly losing his balance. Master and apprentice stood shoulder to shoulder in front of the urinal and stared at the deodorant balls tumbling and rolling under the liquid assault, neither man so much as glancing at the other.

"Who ever heard of having to pay to use a toilet?" he muttered.

"Shifu, you're like a man from Mars. I can't think of anything you don't have to pay for these days," his apprentice said with a shrug. "But it isn't all bad. If not for pay toilets, lower-class people like us would never have the privilege of relieving ourselves in such a high-class place, not even in our dreams."

The apprentice led him over to the sink, where they

washed their hands; then he showed him how to use the blow-dryer. Their mission accomplished, they walked out of the public toilet.

Back in the pedicab, old Ding kept rubbing his rough, blow-dried hands; they'd never felt so moist and smooth.

"Little Hu," he said emotionally, "I've just taken a high-class leak, thanks to you."

"That's funny, Shifu!"

"I owe you one yuan. I'll pay you tomorrow."

"Shifu, you'll say anything for a laugh."

Just before they reached his house, he said, "Stop here."

"We're almost there. I'll take you to your door."

"No, I want to talk to you about something."

"Go ahead."

"Any man who can't make a living and take care of his family is like a woman who can't have children. He can't hold his head up in society."

"You're right, Shifu."

"Which is why I need to go out and find some work."

"That sounds good to me."

"But there are laid-off workers everywhere you look, not counting all those people working on public projects. Just about every job you can think of is taken."

"That's about how things are."

"Little Hu, there's no such thing as a true dead-end, wouldn't you say?"

"Shifu, those are the words of a sage, so they must be true."

"Well, I discovered a path to riches today. Now the only question is, should I do it or not?"

"Shifu, as long as it's not murder or arson you're talking

about, or highway robbery, I don't see any reason why you shouldn't."

"But what I'm talking about, well, it might not be legal. . . ."

"Shifu, don't scare me like that. You know I'm not a brave man."

But once he laid out his plan in detail, Lü Xiaohu said excitedly:

"Shifu, no one but a genius like you could come up with a brilliant idea like that. Now I can see how you were able to invent a two-wheeled, double-shared plow in the 1950s. How could what you're talking about be illegal? If something like that's illegal, well . . . Shifu, this will be a rest stop for lovers, not only civilized, but humane as well. This may not sound good, but you'll be setting up a . . . a sort of pay toilet! Forget your misgivings and go to it, Shifu. Tomorrow I'll get a bunch of guys together to help you put it in shape!"

"Don't tell anyone about this. You're the only one who knows."

"As you say, Shifu."

"That includes my wife."

"Don't you worry, Shifu."

6

He was sitting in the woods between the cemetery and man-made lake, leaning up against a poplar. A little path wound its way up the hill, disappearing from view from time to time. Every once in a while his gaze traveled past the woods up to the edge of the cemetery. He could only see a corner of his little cottage, but it was all right there in his mind.

A few days before, he and Lü Xiaohu had gone back to the factory. After being let in by the gateman, he took advantage of a lifetime of "connections" to pick up discarded sheet metal, rivets, steel plate, and other items. The two men spent the next two days repairing and cleaning up the dilapidated bus hulk. They used the sheet metal to seal up the broken windows, then made doors out of steel plate, with locks on both sides. Once the repairs were made, Lü Xiaohu turned up a bucket of green paint and another of yellow. With the two men slapping on paint, this way and that, a broken-down hulk of an abandoned bus was transformed into something that looked like a military transport in a subtropical jungle. Master and apprentice stepped back to admire their work; the faint smell of paint made them happier than they could have expected.

"Shifu," Lü Xiaohu said, "it's done."

"Yes, it is."

"Should we set off some firecrackers to celebrate?"

"Let's not."

"As soon as the paint dries, you're open for business."

"What do we do if there's trouble, little Hu?"

"Don't sweat it, Shifu. I've got a cousin at the Public Security Bureau."

On the night before he opened for business Ding was so excited he didn't sleep a wink. His wife was so excited she couldn't stop hiccupping. They were both out of bed at four in the morning, and as she prepared his breakfast and lunch, she kept asking him what sort of job he'd found.

"I already told you," he said impatiently. "I'm going to be an advisor to some peasant entrepreneurs in the suburbs."

"I saw you and little Hu whispering back and forth," she said between hiccups. "I doubt you were talking about being an advisor. Don't go getting involved in any shady practice at your age."

"Can't you find something good to say this early in the morning?" he replied angrily. "Come along with me if you don't believe me. You can let those peasant entrepreneurs feast their eyes on your esteemed countenance!"

His comment took the wind out of her sails, and she shut up.

From his vantage point under a tree, he watched a bunch of old folks hard at work on their morning exercises: airing caged birds, strolling, practicing Tai Chi, doing Chi Kung, some voice training. The sight of all those contented people depressed him. If he had a child — son or daughter, it made no difference — he wouldn't be here sitting under a tree early in the morning, laid off or not; he was like the fool who saw a rabbit run into a tree stump and break its neck, then spent his days after that waiting for a second rabbit to do the same. A layer of mist hung over the man-made lake as an orange glow appeared in the east. An old man doing voice exercises seemed to rock the woods:

"Ow-ke — ow-ke —"

Waves of melancholy washed over him, like the ripples on a breezy lake. But only for a moment. A new stage in his life was about to begin, and the new life, like the woman who bought the little pigs, filled his mind with too many lustful thoughts for him to get sentimental. In the hour or so before sunup, the woods were filled with the songs and chirps of birds; the air had a minty quality that cleansed his lungs and lifted his spirits. It didn't take long for him to see how wrong he'd been to come out so early. At this time of day, only old folks were out, and they preferred the area around the lake to the cemetery; even if they came to the cemetery, they weren't the clientele he was waiting for. But that's all right, he consoled himself. I'll count this as my morning exercise. After breathing the foul factory air for decades, it's time I gave my lungs a break with some fresh air. Picking up his camp stool, he strolled through the woods and around the cemetery to familiarize himself with the area. The discarded birth control paraphernalia he spotted on the ground made him more confident than ever that he'd chosen the right path.

Around noon, several couples in bathing suits and large towels draped over their shoulders walked over from the lake, looking very much like lovers in search of a spot to get naked together. But when they passed by him, he suddenly became tongue-tied, and all those catchy phrases that Lü Xiaohu had created and that he had committed to memory stuck in his throat. Hearing the sounds the couples made in the dense woods, all roughly the same, but discernibly individual, was like seeing his own folding money swept away by the wind, filling his heart with a mixture of regret and despondence.

That night he went to see his apprentice and, with considerable embarrassment, told him what had happened during the day.

"Shifu," Lü Xiaohu said with a laugh, "what's there for a laid-off worker to be embarrassed about?"

He scratched his head. "Little Hu, you know I'm a grade-seven worker who's spent most of his life in the company of iron and steel. I never thought I'd come to this in my old age."

"If you don't mind my saying so, Shifu, you still don't know what it means to be hungry. If that day comes, you'll know that in a contest between face and belly, your belly will win every time!"

"I see what you're saying, but for some reason I can't open my mouth."

"It's not your fault," his apprentice said with another laugh. "You're a grade-seven worker, after all. Tell you what, Shifu, I've got a plan. . . ."

At noon the following day, old Ding returned to the spot he'd picked out the day before, carrying a piece of wood on his back. Anyone entering the cemetery from the hill had to pass this way. Though it was a secluded area, it was surrounded by open space. From where he sat, in the mottled shadows of a tall poplar, he had a clear view of people swimming in the lake. With all the birds off somewhere, the only sound was the constant chirping of crickets, which sent their cool droppings down on him like raindrops.

Finally, a couple came walking up the path. They were in full view: the woman was wearing a sky-blue bikini, her milky white skin glistening between the leafy shadows; the man wore a pair of stretch trunks and had a hairy chest and legs. Giggling as their hands roamed all over each other, they drew nearer and nearer; the sight of all that cleavage and the mole on her belly made old Ding feel like a voyeur. He also noticed with disgust that the man's belly button protruded instead of sinking in and that his trunks looked as if he'd hidden a potato in the front. When they were only a few feet from him, he picked up the piece of wood at his feet and raised it up high enough to cover his face, which felt as if it were on fire. The red lettering was aimed at the couple. He watched the woman's long, slender legs and the man's hairy ones stop in their tracks and listened as the man read the sign aloud:

"A quiet, secluded, safe cottage in the woods. Ten yuan per hour, includes two soft drinks."

The woman giggled.

"Hey, there, old man, where's this cottage of yours?" the man asked audaciously.

Old Ding lowered the board to reveal the top half of his face. "There," he stammered, "over there."

"Can we take a look?" The man grinned at the woman and said, "I am a little thirsty."

The woman gave him a seductive look out of the corner of her eye. "You can die of thirst for all I care!"

With a sly look and a smile at the woman, the man turned to old Ding and said:

"Take us over to see the place, old man."

He stood, noticeably agitated, picked up his stool, put the board under his arm and led them through the cemetery to the abandoned bus.

"This is your little cottage?" the man exclaimed. "It's a damned iron coffin!"

Old Ding unlocked the brass lock and swung the heavy door open.

The man bent at the waist and went inside.

"Hey, Ping'er," he shouted, "it's goddamned cool in here!"

The woman looked askance at old Ding, a slight blush on her face, before sticking her head in to take a look. Then she went in.

The man stuck his head out. "It's too dark in here. I can't see a thing!"

Old Ding handed him a disposable lighter.

"There's a candle on the table," he said.

The candle cast its yellow light on the inside of the bus. He watched as the woman took a drink from the soda bottle in her hand. Her still wet hair streamed down her back like a horse's tail, nearly covering her high, jutting buttocks.

The man stepped out of the bus and made a sweep of the area. "Say, old man," he asked in a soft voice, "do you guarantee nobody comes around here?"

"There's a lock inside," he said. "You've got my guarantee."

"We'd like to take a nap," the man said, "and we don't want any interruptions."

Old Ding nodded.

The man went back inside.

Old Ding heard the door being locked.

After walking over to a little grove of locust trees, he looked at his ancient pocket watch, in its metal casing, like a coach on the sidelines. At first, there was no sound inside the bus, but about ten minutes later, the woman began to shout. Because the bus was sealed up so tightly, the shouts sounded as if they came up from under the ground. Old Ding was on pins and needles, as images of the woman's tender white skin swirled inside his head. He thumped his own leg and muttered:

"Don't be thinking about things like that, you old fart!"

But the woman's pale flesh had attached itself to his brain and wouldn't let go. Then the smiling face and cleavage of the woman buying piglets came to join the party.

Fifty minutes later, the steel door swung open and out stepped the woman, now dressed in street clothes. Her face was red, her eyes bright, the look of a hen that's just laid an egg. She glanced off to the side, as if she didn't even know he was there, and walked off toward the cemetery. Then the man emerged, a bath towel draped over his arm and a bottle of soda in his hand. He walked up to the man and said timidly:

"Fifty minutes . . ."

"How much?"

"It's up to you . . ."

The man, also in street clothes, reached into his pocket and pulled out a fifty-yuan bill. He handed it to old Ding, whose hand shook; his heart was racing.

"I don't have any change," he said.

"Keep it," the man said airily. "We're coming back tomorrow."

Crushing the bill in his fist, he thought he might burst into tears.

"Old man, you're really something!" the man said as he tossed the empty bottle away. "You ought to stock the place with condoms," he said softly. "That and some cigarettes and beer. Then double the price."

Old Ding responded with a deep bow.

7

Acting on the man's suggestion, he outfitted his little love cottage with everything couples might need for their trysts, as well as beer, soft drinks, and snacks of dried fish slices and preserved plums. The first time he went to the pharmacy for condoms, he was so embarrassed he couldn't hold his head up or make clear what it was he wanted, to the utter contempt of the young woman behind the counter. As he slinked out of the store with his prophylactic purchase, he heard her say to another clerk behind her:

"Hey, who'd have thought an old geezer like that still had use for those . . ."

But as his business grew with each passing day, so did his nerve and his business sense. No longer flushed with embarrassment when he made his purchases at the pharmacy, he even tried to get the clerk to come down on the price. Brazenly, she remarked:

"Old man, if you're not some kind of sex fiend, you must be engaged in black market trade in condoms."

"I'm both a sex fiend and a black marketer," he shot back naughtily, looking directly at the woman's scarlet lips.

Over the three months of summer, he netted forty-eight hundred yuan. And as his purse grew fatter, he grew more cheerful and physically robust by the day. Joints that had turned rusty limbered up, as if newly lubricated, and his eyes, which had seemed frozen in place, were now filled with life. And once his eyes and ears grew attuned to the sights and sounds of his new environment, the torch of intimacy, long extinguished, ignited anew. After he had taken his wife to bed more than once, to her incredible astonishment, she asked him, "What sort of tonic have you been taking, you old fart? Trying to kill yourself?"

At ten-thirty every morning, he climbed onto his bike and rode over to the cottage, where he first cleaned the place up, dumping all the trash from the previous day into a plastic bag, which he made sure to double-knot. As someone who placed great importance on social conscience, he would never throw his trash just anywhere; no, he carried it into town and properly disposed of it in a trash receptacle. After cleaning up the place, he replenished his stock of drinks, snacks, and other items. That done, he locked the door, picked up his stool, and found a place to wait for the day's clientele, leisurely smoking a cigarette to pass the time. His taste in cigarettes had improved. In the past, he'd smoked only unfiltered Golden City, but now he'd switched to filtered Flying Swallows. In the past, he couldn't bring himself to look his clients in the eye; now he studied them intently. As he gained more experience, he found he could pretty much predict which couples were likely to use his service and which were not. Most of his customers were birds on the prowl, intent on enjoying each other's bodies illicitly; but once in a while a curious married couple or two people in a committed relationship dropped by. There were at least a dozen repeat customers; he always gave them a cut-rate price, usually 20 percent off, but sometimes as much as 50 percent. Some of his customers were the talkative type, and after they'd finished their business, they'd talk his ear off; others were the bashful type, who took off as soon as they'd handed over the money. His storehouse of knowledge about the sex life of young couples was greatly enriched, thanks to his ears alone. The endless variety of sounds, male and female, emerging from the cottage created at least as many pictures in his mind, sort of like throwing open a window onto a vast panorama. One seemingly sickly couple bounced and thudded around the bus so noisily you'd have thought it was a pair of mating elephants in there, not copulating humans. Then there was the couple who started out by shouting and carrying on and ended by slugging it out and smashing beer bottles. But there was nothing he could do about it, since breaking in on them at a time like that could bring nothing but bad luck. The man emerged with a bloody head, the woman with her hair looking like a rat's nest. He felt sorry enough for them to give them a freebie, but the man actually grandstanded by tossing a hundred-yuan note on the ground before strutting off. When he ran after him to give him change, the man turned and spat in his face. The man had thin, sparse eyebrows, sunken eyes, and a mean look; one glare sent old Ding scurrying off abjectly.

With the arrival of autumn, the poplar leaves began to fall and pine needles darkened. Fewer and fewer people came to swim in the lake, seriously affecting his business; but no day passed without a few clients, especially on Sundays and holidays. This gave him a chance to take it easy, and income was income, even though there might be less of it. It all added up. He came down with a cold about then, but that didn't stop him from going to work. Not wanting to part with his money for cold preparations, he let his wife cook up a pot of ginger soup. He drank down three bowlfuls of the stuff, then covered himself from head to toe and sweated it out. You couldn't ask for a better folk remedy. His plan was to save up as much money as possible for his old age while he was still able. Now that the factory had given him all the severance pay he had coming, the government couldn't be counted on, since even teachers' pay was slow in coming and the government had to take out loans to pay cadres' salaries. It was every man for himself, not all that different from grabbing what you could after a natural disaster. There were times when he felt uncomfortable, uncertain if he was a saint or a sinner. One night he dreamed that the police came for him, and he woke up in a cold sweat, his heart racing. He met with his apprentice, Lü Xiaohu, in a quiet little wine shop, and told him what was bothering him.

"Shifu," Hu said, "you're not getting goofy on me again, are you? Don't tell me you think your cottage is the only reason those people do it! They'll keep doing it, with or without your cottage. In the woods, in the cemetery, somewhere. Young folks these days are always talking about returning to nature and free love, and who are we to say there's anything wrong with that? They're people, just like us. I told you at the beginning, just pretend you've set up a public toilet in the wild, for which you have every right to charge a modest fee. Shifu, you're head and shoulders above those people who flood the market with their phony alcohol and fake medicine. You have absolutely no reason to be so hard on yourself. Being on good terms with money is more important than trying to be a good son. Without money, you can forget about a loving mother and father, and even your old lady will turn her back on you. Shifu, show some spunk and get on with your business. If there's any trouble, just leave everything to me!"

Old Ding could find nothing wrong with his apprentice's argument. He's right, he concluded. Sure, there was nothing saintly about what he was doing, but one saint was plenty in this world. Any more was just asking for trouble. The last thing

Ding Shikou wanted was to be a saint. Besides, he couldn't even if he wanted to. Ding Shikou, he was thinking, you're doing the government a big favor. Being the master of a love cottage in the woods may not bring you honor, but it's a lot better than causing a scene in front of the government headquarters. This thought brought a smile to his face, which flabbergasted his wife, who was shucking peanuts at the table.

"What are you smiling about, you old fart?" she asked him. "Do you have any idea how scary a smile like that looks?"

"Scary?"

"Yes, scary."

"Well, today that's exactly what I want to do, scare you."

"Just what do you have in mind, you old fart?" she asked as she backed away, holding a handful of peanut shells. Lightning split the sky outside, heralding a downpour. Cool, damp air seeped into the room, causing the atmosphere inside to actually heat up. He removed his clothes as he bore down on his wife, tossing them behind him; she cowered against the wall, her face turning scarlet, her normally gloomy eyes shining like those of a girl in her prime. Cornered, she flung the peanut shells in his face. "You old fart," she muttered, "the older you get, the crazier you are . . . the middle of the day . . . what do you think you're doing. . . . The lord of thunder and mother of lightning are looking at you." He grabbed her around the waist and bent her backward. "You old fart!" she screamed. "Old fart . . . not so hard . . . you're going to break me in half. . . ."

In order to guard against any unforeseen trouble, Ding deposited his earnings under a phony name and hid the passbook in a hole in the wall, which he sealed with two layers of paper.

After the winter solstice, the temperature began to drop and there were no clients for two or three days in a row. He rode over to his cottage around noon. Frost clung to the fallen leaves on the ground. The dark yellow sun cast precious little heat. He sat under a tree for a while, until his fingers and toes turned icy cold. The lake was quiet, deserted, except for a man walking in circles by the water's edge, gauze wrapped around his neck. He was a man engaged in a life-and-death struggle with cancer, a bit of a celebrity around town, owing to the fight he was putting up; the local TV station had aired a segment on his struggle. The station had sent a crew down to the lake to film the story, scaring the hell out of Ding. Just to be safe, he'd climbed a tree and perched up there like a bird for over two hours.

After that incident, a fire inspection team had come to the area, frightening him half to death. This time he'd hidden behind a tree and waited there with his heart in his mouth. One by one the men had walked past his little cottage, but with no visible reaction, as if it were just another of nature's creations. The sole exception was a fat guy who had walked behind the cottage to release a stream of yellow piss. Ding could actually smell it. Our leaders are suffering from too much internal heat, he thought to himself. The fat guy looked to be getting on in years, but he pissed like a youngster: sucking in his gut, he formed a wet circle on the sheet-metal side of the bus, then another and another; but before he could complete the fourth circle, the stream broke off. After taking his young man's leak, the fat guy rapped loudly on one of the sheet-metal window coverings before buttoning his fly and waddling quickly off to catch up with his partners. Just those two frightening episodes.

The chilled air under the tree was too much for Ding, so he got up and moved into the bus to sit down and have a smoke.

After carefully extinguishing his cigarette, he closed his eyes and roughly calculated how much he'd made over the six months or so he'd been in business. The results were gratifying. He decided to come back tomorrow, and if there were still no clients, he'd close up shop until the following spring. If I can keep this up for five years, I'll be in great shape for old age.

He rode out to the cottage early the next morning. Cold overnight winds had nearly denuded the trees; there were hardly any leaves left on the poplar branches, while those on the few oak trees scattered among the pines held on and turned a golden color. As they rustled in the wind, they looked like yellow butterflies swarming amid the branches. He came equipped with a snakeskin-patterned sack and a steel-tipped wooden staff. He picked up all the litter in the broad vicinity of the little cottage, not for any monetary gain, but out of a sense of obligation. He was a beneficiary of the best that society had to offer. After tying off the trash bag, he placed it on his bicycle rack, then went into the cottage to gather up the assortment of articles. The caw of a solitary crow outside made his heart skip a beat. Taking a look out the door, he spotted a man and a woman walking his way up the gray path from the little hill behind the factory.

8

The couple, middle-aged, stopped in front of the cottage. It was half-past noon. The man, his hands thrust into the pockets of his gray windbreaker, was quite tall. The wind behind him billowed the cuffs of his pants and exposed his lower calves. The woman was shorter, but not by much; calling upon his decades of experience in sizing up lengths of iron, old Ding guessed that she was in the neighborhood of five-five or five-six. She was wearing a purple down parka over a pair of light blue jeans and white lambskin shoes. Since neither of them was wearing a hat, their hair was at the mercy of the wind, and the woman frequently reached up to pull her hair back out of her face. As they drew up to the cottage, they subconsciously increased the distance between them, which only served to strengthen the impression that they were lovers, and probably had been for many years. When old Ding saw the cold, pained expression on the man's face and the look of an indignant woman on hers, he knew exactly what was going on between them, as if he'd just finished reading their dossiers.

He decided to stay open for one final pair of clients, not because of the money, but because his heart went out to them.

The man spoke to old Ding in front of the cottage, while the woman stood with her back to the door, her hands in the pockets of her parka, as she absentmindedly kicked at some leaves on the ground.

"It sure turned cold today," the man said. "All of a sudden, like. Not normal."

"On TV they say it's a cold front down from Siberia," old Ding said, reminding himself that he ought to get rid of the old black-and-white TV at home.

"So this is the famous lovers' cottage," the man said. "I hear it's the brainchild of the Chief of Police's father-in-law."

Old Ding just smiled and shook his head, which could have meant almost anything.

"Actually," the man said, "all we're looking for is a quiet spot so we can talk."

Old Ding gave him an understanding smile, picked up his stool, and headed over to the locust grove without so much as a backward glance.

Sunbeams burst from a gray cloud, flooding the woods with dazzling light. The locust tree seemed covered with a layer of tinfoil, glittery and magical. As he leaned against the springy limbs of the tree, powerful gusts of a northeast wind felt as if they had turned his spine into cold metal. The man stepped into the cottage, bent at the waist. The woman stood off to one side of the doorway, her head lowered, as if deep in thought. The man emerged from the cottage and walked up behind the woman to whisper something. There was no change in her demeanor. So the man reached out and gently tugged at the hem of her coat. She squirmed, a childish movement, like a little girl's display of temper. The man rested his hand on her shoulder, and even though she continued to squirm, she did not shake off his hand. So he pressed down and turned her toward him; she put up mild resistance, but ultimately turned to face him. Then, with both hands on her shoulders, he spoke to her — to the top of her head, actually. At last, he ushered her into the cottage.

Hidden from view beneath the locust tree, old Ding smiled. The metal door closed with a soft click; he then heard the barely perceptible turning of the lock. With that sound, the little cottage became another dead object in the wintry woods, touched from time to time by the sun's cold and desolate rays, giving off brief bursts of murky reflections. Tan-feathered sparrows shitting on the roof of the cottage flitted back and

42

forth, raising a chorus of chirpings. Monstrous, bloated gray clouds sped across the sky, their dark shadows skittering across the wooded ground. He looked at his pocket watch — it was one o'clock. He didn't expect them to be in there long, probably no more than an hour. He'd been about to go home for lunch when these last two "uninvited guests" had showed up. He was getting hungry, and cold, but he'd have to wait them out before heading home. They were, after all, paying by the hour, so he had no right to ask them to leave before they were ready. Some of the couples stayed inside for up to three hours. Up till now, he'd have been happy if his clients had locked themselves inside and slept for eight or ten hours. But with the wind chilling him to the bone and the pangs of hunger growing stronger, he wished they would finish their business quickly and come out. He passed the time by digging a little hole in the ground in front of him with his walking stick, then lighting up a cigarette. Always conscious of the fire danger in a wooded area, he carefully flicked his ashes into the hole.

He'd been sitting under the tree for about half an hour when he heard muted sobs from inside the cottage. A gust of wind set the leaves rustling loudly enough to swallow up the sobs. But as soon as the wind died down, the sobs found their way back into his ears. He sighed sympathetically. This was the sort of romance lovers like that deserved; theirs was a classical, tragic love, like cucumbers in a pickling vat — all salt, no sugar. Young folks these days have gotten away from that. When they're in the cottage, they take advantage of every second, going at it hot and heavy. They scream lecherously, they moan, some of them fill the air with obscenities that make the birds blush. They all do the same thing, but the way they go

43

about it couldn't be more different. By studying the intimate sounds of the men and women, he gained an understanding into changes in people's concepts. Deep down in his heart, he preferred a tearful love, which seemed more dramatic, somehow. As he listened to the sobs and whimpers, he thought about their story: it had to be a sentimental one, a romantic tragedy. For a number of reasons, marriage was not in the cards for them. Maybe, after being separated by a vast distance, this man and woman had come together to meet secretly. Viewed from that angle, he thought, I'm actually a good Samaritan.

He let his thoughts ramble for another hour before getting to his feet to limber up his achy joints and massage his nearly frozen earlobes. It was time to pack up and go home. He decided that the only way to feel good about how things had worked out was to charge them a nominal fee, then stop at the Lanzhou Noodle Restaurant in town for a bowl of beef noodles. The mere thought of those noodles had his stomach rumbling and his teeth chattering. He was damned hungry, and damned cold. It was unseasonably cold, abnormally cold, ridiculously cold, colder than the coldest days of winter last year. The woman's sobs had stopped, leaving the metal cottage perfectly still, quiet as a graveyard. A crow with a piece of intestine in its beak flew up from some distant place and landed in its nest in a poplar tree.

Another hour passed, and the little cottage remained still as death. The clouds kept gathering, and signs of dusk began to settle around the woods. What's going on? he asked himself silently. They didn't look that robust to me. Could they have fallen asleep in there? No, that's impossible! There's nothing in there but a slat bed covered by a straw mat. No mattress and no blankets. It's cold enough outside, even with a bit of weak sunlight; but once that door is closed, the cottage turns into cold storage. So what are they doing in there? He held off as long as he could before walking up to the door and coughing loudly as a signal for them to wrap things up and come out. No response from inside. Don't tell me they vanished into thin air like the goblins in *Roll Call of the Gods*? No, that's just some supernatural novel. Could they have turned into mosquitoes like the immortal monkey and flown out the window? Impossible, another supernatural story! They couldn't have. . . . A murky and utterly terrifying scene suddenly flashed before his eyes. His arms and legs began to quake. My god, not that! If that's what's happened, forget about my road to riches. I'll be lucky if I don't wind up in prison. All of a sudden, nothing else mattered. He raised his hand and knocked lightly on the door.

Rap rap rap.

Then he knocked harder.

Thump thump thump!

Then he pounded with his fist.

Pow pow pow!

Then he pounded with all his might and shouted at the top of his lungs:

Pow pow pow! Hey, come out of there! *Pow pow pow!* What are you doing in there? A trickle of blood oozed from a split between his thumb and finger. Still there was no sound from inside the cottage; for a moment, he wondered if his memory was failing him. Did a couple like that really go inside?

But then the woman's pale oval face suddenly floated in front of his eyes, incredibly lifelike. Her black, mysterious eyes were filled with a haunting look. She had a pointy chin and a bean-sized black mole by the corner of her mouth, out of which grew one long, curly black hair. The image of the man was just as clear. His raised raincoat collar covered his cheeks. He had a high nose, dark chin, and bushy eyebrows; his eyes were gloomy, he had one gold tooth. . . .

No doubt about it, a cold, hard fact: about three hours ago, a sorrowful middle-aged couple stepped inside this abandoned bus, converted into a little woodland cottage; but now they weren't making a sound, and he just knew that the worst thing imaginable had happened. Bad luck was like a foul-smelling honey bucket, and it had just been tipped over on him. His legs buckled, sending him slumping to the ground right in front of the door.

After about as long as it takes to smoke a cigarette, he managed to climb to his feet. He took several turns around the cottage, banging his hand against the metal skin from time to time.

"Hey, you good people," he raged and pleaded, "wake up and come out of there. I'll give you every penny I made all summer, okay? I'll get down on my knees and kowtow to you, okay? You bastards, you animals, aren't you afraid lightning will strike you dead for taking advantage of an old man? You adulterers, you fornicators, whore, whoremonger, you'll come to a terrible end. I'll call you Daddy, okay? And I'll call you Mommy, okay? Daddy, Mommy, dear ancestors, be merciful and come out of there. I'm a sixty-year-old laid-off factory worker with a wife at home who suffers from stomach problems. That's bad enough, so don't go adding frost to a layer of snow. If dying's what you want, do it somewhere else, not in my cottage. Go hang yourselves from one of those trees, or go drown yourselves in the lake, or go lie down on the railroad tracks. There are all kinds of places to go kill yourselves, so why choose my little cottage to do it? I can tell you're people of means and status, at least a section chief, if not a bureau chief. Is something like this worth dying over? Dying like that is about as meaningful as a bird's feather. It's not worth it. If even people like you don't want to go on living, what about us folks from the lower classes? Bureau Chief, Section Chief, use your head and put yourself in my place. Come out, please come out. . . ."

He yelled himself hoarse, and still not a sound from inside the cottage. Crows returning to their nests as the sun was setting noisily circled in the sky above the poplars, like a gathering cloud. He picked up a big rock and tried to smash down the metal door. A resounding clang ended in the rock splitting in two; the door suffered no damage. So he hunched up his shoulder and used his body as a battering ram. The door barely moved, but he was thrown back at least three meters and sat down hard on the ground. His shoulder hurt like hell. He could barely raise his arm. It felt like his clavicle was broken.

9

He rode his clunky bicycle down from the mountain in a daze, never once hitting the brake, as if death were the only solution. He was heading straight into a northeast wind that billowed his coat and nearly froze his abdomen as the wind whistled past his ears; it was as if he were riding the clouds and soaring through the mist. The garbage bag on the rack behind him blew open, sending soiled paper and plastic bags into the air with a loud *whoosh*. As he skirted the lakeshore, he didn't see the cancer-battling celebrity. A flock of gray swans wheeled in the air, as if looking for a spot to land on the frozen lake, the ice blanketed with dust and dirt. He rode into town, totally numb. The streetlights were already on; a constant explosion of broken glass drove his heart up into his throat. A police car cruised past, lights flashing, siren off; he nearly fell off his bike in terror.

Muddle-headed though he was, he managed to make his way to the door of his apprentice, Lü Xiaohu, and had just raised his hand to knock when he spotted a drawing pasted on the door; it was a sketch of a boy with anger in his eyes. Old Ding turned to get out of there just as he saw his apprentice coming up the hallway carrying a plucked chicken. The sight of the dead chicken's pimply skin in the murky light raised goose bumps on his skin. His legs buckled, causing shooting pains in his newly healed broken leg, and he sat down hard on the steps. Lü Xiaohu stopped dead in his tracks.

"Shifu," he asked anxiously, "what are you doing here?"

Like a little boy who's been picked on, then suddenly sees his daddy, old Ding felt his lips begin to quiver and tears spill from his eyes.

"What's the matter, Shifu?" his apprentice asked as he rushed up to help old Ding to his feet. "Has something happened?"

His knees buckled, and he knelt at the feet of his disciple.

"Little Hu," he sobbed, "something terrible . . ."

Quickly opening his apartment door, little Hu dragged him inside and sat him down on the sofa.

"Shifu, what's happened? Your wife hasn't died, has she?"

"No," he said weakly. "It's much worse than that. . . ."

"Tell me, what is it?" Little Hu was getting worried. "Shifu, tell me before I die of anxiety."

"Little Hu," he sobbed, wiping his tears, "I'm in big trouble. . . ."

"What is it? Tell me!"

"A man and woman went in around noon today, and they still haven't come out. . . ."

"So? Just collect more money from them." Little Hu breathed a sigh of relief. "This is good news."

"What do you mean, good news? They died in there. . . ."

"Died?" Little Hu was stunned; he nearly dropped the hot vacuum bottle he had in one hand. "How'd that happen?"

"I'm not sure. . . ."

"Have you seen their bodies?"

"No."

"Then how do you know they're dead?"

"They must be . . . they went in over three hours ago, and at first I heard the woman sob. Then no more sound." He showed his apprentice his injured hand. "I tried to break down the door, I pounded on the windows, I shouted, and hurt myself doing it, but no sound inside, not even a whisper. . . ."

Little Hu laid down his vacuum bottle and sat on a stool across from the sofa. He took out a pack of cigarettes, put one in his mouth and lit it. With his head lowered, he took a deep drag, then looked up. "Shifu," he said, "take it easy." He took out another cigarette, handed it to old Ding, and lit it for him. "Maybe they fell asleep. That sort of activity can tire a person out."

Old Ding nervously rubbed his knees with his hands as he sat there gazing hopefully into the eyes of his apprentice.

"My fine young apprentice, you don't need to try to reassure me," he said sorrowfully. "I knocked till my knuckles were bloody and yelled myself hoarse. I made enough noise to wake the dead. But nothing stirred inside, nothing. . . ."

"Couldn't they have slipped out while you weren't looking? That sounds plausible to me. Shifu, you should know that there's nothing people won't do to get out of paying what they owe."

Ding shook his head. "That's not possible, absolutely impossible. First of all, the door is bolted from the inside. Besides, I never took my eyes off the place. I'd have seen a pair of rats scurrying out of there, let alone a pair of full-sized humans."

"Rats, you say. How about this?" Little Hu said. "They tunneled their way out."

"My fine apprentice," old Ding said, his voice cracking tearfully, "forget your wacky theories and help me figure out what to do. I beg you!"

Little Hu lowered his head and puffed away on his cigarette. Deep lines creased his brow. Old Ding stared at his apprentice without blinking, waiting to hear his ideas. Little Hu looked up.

"Shifu," he said, "I think we just say to hell with it. You've earned a tidy sum this year. Now we wait till next spring and come up with another money-making scheme."

"Little Hu, we're talking about the loss of two lives. . . ."

"So? That's not our fault," he said angrily. "Once they decided to die, there was nothing we could do about it. What kind of fuck-ups were they?"

"They looked like educated people to me, maybe party officials."

"That's even more reason to stay clear of them. With people like that, you know they're having an extramarital affair. No one will shed a tear over their deaths."

"But," he stammered, "what if they tie this to me? As the saying goes, you can't bury bodies in the snowy ground. The police will know it was me right off."

"What are you getting at? Don't tell me you're thinking of going to the police yourself."

"Little Hu, I've given this a lot of thought. You know what they say: the ugly bride has to face her in-laws sooner or later."

"Are you really thinking of going to the police?"

"Maybe, they might still be able to save them."

"Shifu, this is pretty much the same as setting yourself on fire!"

"My fine apprentice, didn't you say you have a cousin who works at the Public Security Bureau? Will you take me to see him?"

"Shifu!"

"I beg you, I need your cousin's help. If I did nothing, I don't think I could get another good night's sleep ever again."

"Shifu," Little Hu said in a somber tone of voice, "have you given any thought to possible consequences? What you've been engaged in will seem sordid to people, and it won't take much digging to find a law that'll send you away for a couple of years. And even if that doesn't happen, you can look forward to a hefty fine. And when those people fine you, you know you've been fined. I wouldn't be surprised if the money you've earned over an entire summer, plus the fall, won't be enough to pay it off."

"I have to live with that," old Ding admitted painfully. "I don't want that money. From now on, I'll go begging before I do anything like this again."

"And what if you're looking at jail time?" his apprentice asked him.

"That's why I want you to speak to your cousin," he said weakly, his head sagging. "If it's jail time I'm looking at, I'll just go get some rat poison and put an end to everything."

"Shifu! Shifu!" Little Hu said. "All that stuff about a cousin with the police, I just said that to boost your confidence."

Old Ding stood there woodenly for a moment, then sighed and rose shakily to his feet. After carefully stubbing out his cigarette in the ashtray, he looked over at his former apprentice, who was staring at the wall, his head cocked to one side, and said, "Then I won't trouble you anymore."

He turned and hobbled to the door.

"Shifu, where are you going?"

He looked back over his shoulder.

"Little Hu," he said, "you and I worked together for a while. After I'm gone, if it's not too much trouble, would you check on my wife from time to time? If it is, don't worry about it. . . ."

He reached out and opened the door. A cold wind filling the hallway hit him full in the face. He shivered as he reached out to hold on to the dusty banister and walked off into the dark.

"Wait up, Shifu." He turned and saw his apprentice standing in the doorway. Light streaming out of the apartment made his face appear to be brushed with gold dust. He heard him say, "I'll take you to see my cousin."

10

They squeezed into a phone booth, with wind whistling all around them, to call the cousin at home. Whoever answered the phone said he was on duty at the station house. Old Ding's former apprentice said happily:

"Great, Shifu. Do you know why I didn't want to take you to see him? You have no idea how arrogant his wife is. If a poor relation like me goes to their house, her nose is bent out of shape, and her face turns all weird. Like any dog, the bitch sees people like us as her inferior. It's more than I can take. We may be poor in material wealth, but not in our ideals. Isn't that so?"

Old Ding said emotionally:

"Little Hu, I'm sorry to put you through all this."

"But my cousin's a great guy. A little hen-pecked, that's all." Then, in a singsong voice, he added, "When a man's wife rules, he sleeps with the mules!"

They stopped first at a sundries shop to buy two cartons of China-brand cigarettes. Old Ding went for his wallet, but his former apprentice pushed his hand away.

"Shifu," he said, "I'll take care of this. You can't afford it."

When he saw how much the cigarettes cost, he gritted his teeth and said, no matter how much it pained him:

"I should be paying for this, little Hu."

"Just leave things to me for now."

When they walked into the police station, old Ding reached out involuntarily and held on to the hem of his former apprentice's shirt. He felt cold all over, and his palms were sweaty. As it turned out, one of the two duty policemen was the cousin, a young man with slitty eyes and a long neck. He picked up his pen and wrote down everything they told him in a notebook.

"That's it?" he remarked impatiently, tapping the notebook with the tip of his pen.

"That's it. . . ."

"Quite a fertile imagination," he said coldly, looking at old Ding out of the corner of his eye. "Made quite a bundle, did you?"

He opened his mouth to speak, but nothing came out.

"Cousin," old Ding's apprentice said, smiling broadly as he laid the plastic bag containing the cigarettes in front of the policeman, "won't you please look into this for the shifu here? If those two took sleeping pills, we might still be able to rescue them. Ding Shifu taught me everything I know. He's a provincial model worker who once had his picture taken with Deputy Governor Yu. But when he was laid off recently, this was the only way he knew to put food on the table."

"And what if they took rat poison?" The cousin looked at his watch, got to his feet, and said to the other duty policeman, who was playing computer games off in the corner, "Little Sun, I'm going over to the lake to look into a possible suicide. You take care of things here."

After visiting the bathroom and picking up all the equipment he'd need, the cousin went out to the garage and returned with a motorized three-wheeler. Once old Ding and his apprentice were seated, they drove out of the station compound.

It was right around dinnertime, but it felt much later, owing possibly to the chill in the air and the paucity of traffic.

With the vehicle's lights flashing and siren blaring, they sped along, with old Ding clinging to the icy railing, his heart in his throat, just waiting for him to open his mouth and spit it out.

They were soon in the outskirts of town, where the road quality began to deteriorate, although the cousin fought the impulse to slow down, as if to demonstrate his driving skills; the three-wheeler was now more like a bucking bronco. Old Ding was bouncing around so badly, his poor tailbone felt as if it were being pricked by needles.

Once they were on the asphalt road skirting the man-made lake, the cousin had no choice but to slow down, since the surface was fraught with serious bumps and hollows. He skillfully negotiated the course, but couldn't avoid all the hazards. Once, the three-wheeler stalled as they came perilously close to flipping over.

"Goddamned corruption road!" he cursed. "They paved it less than a year ago, and look at it now!"

Old Ding and his apprentice climbed down off the three-wheeler and pushed it down the road. When they reached the edge of the cemetery, they had to leave it before going any farther. The headlight pierced the inky darkness and illuminated a narrow strip of the cemetery and surrounding trees.

"Where is it?" the cousin asked coldly.

He tried to answer, but his tongue seemed petrified, and he merely grunted. His apprentice pointed in the direction of the cemetery. "Over there."

The three-wheeler's headlight lit up the little path through the cemetery, but it was clear that they'd have to walk. So the cousin turned off the light, reached into his backpack and took out a flashlight that ran on three double-A batteries. Flicking it on to light the way down the gray path through the trees, he said impatiently:

"Let's go. You lead the way."

So old Ding jumped out in front in an instinctive attempt to get on the cousin's good side. He heard his apprentice say from behind:

"Cousin, the vehicle . . ."

"How's that? Afraid someone might come by and steal it?" He laughed snidely. "Who but a fucking idiot would be out on a cold night like this?"

With the cousin's flashlight jumping from the tips of the trees to the cemetery ahead, old Ding had trouble keeping his footing, like an old horse with failing eyesight. The path threaded its twisting way through the cemetery, the surface covered by a thick carpet of dead leaves that crackled under their feet. The northeast wind had died down; there was a chilled, eerie quality to the air above the extraordinarily quiet cemetery, except for the human footsteps on the crackling leaves, a sound that sent shivers through the heart. Something icy cold fell on old Ding's face, like raindrops, but not really. Then he saw white floating objects in the flashlight's beam.

"It's snowing!" he said with a trace of genuine excitement.

The cousin corrected him in a chiding tone:

"That isn't snow, it's sleet!"

"Cousin," the apprentice said, "how come you know so much?"

With a contemptuous snort, the cousin said:

"You people think that cops are all stupid, don't you?"

"Not for a minute," the apprentice said with an ingratiating smile. "There might be stupid cops on the force, but you're certainly not one of them. I heard my aunt say once that you could read more than two hundred characters at the age of five."

The cousin's flashlight lit up the tip of a tall poplar, startling some crows in a nest. With caws and chirps, two of the birds flew out of the nest and flapped their wings in the beam of light; one banged into the trunk of the tree, the other flew into a magpie's nest, leading to some mighty squawks. Cousin turned off his flashlight and grumbled:

"Goddamned birds, I ought to blow you all away!"

They walked up to the abandoned bus hulk, which looked like a sleeping monster in the umbrella of light. By then the warring crows and magpies had returned to their own nests, returning the woods to silence. The sleet was coming down more heavily now, making a rustling noise in the night air, sort of like the sound of silkworms munching on mulberry leaves. Cousin shone his light all over the cottage.

"Inside?" he asked.

Old Ding felt his apprentice's eyes on him in the darkness and sputtered out an answer:

"Yes, inside . . ."

"Damn, you sure know how to find a spot."

Flashlight in hand, the cousin walked up to the door and gave it a kick. To everyone's surprise, it swung open. Old Ding's eyes followed the beam of light as it moved through the inside of the cottage, like taking inventory of his personal effects. He saw the bed and the straw mat and coarse toilet paper on top of it; the three-legged wooden table against the "wall" in the corner, with its two bottles of beer and three of soda, all of them dusty, two red candles lying next to the beer bottles and another short one, standing up; the dirty melted wax on the table top and the plastic chamber pot; and an anonymous pornographic chalk drawing on the "wall." The beam lingered on the drawing for a moment, then continued on its way. It landed finally on old Ding's face, as the cousin turned and asked him angrily:

"Ding Shifu, what's this all about?"

The light blinded him, so he tried to shield his eyes with his arm as he stammered in his own defense:

"I wasn't lying, I swear to heaven I wasn't lying."

The cousin said cynically, "There are people who walk mules and people who walk horses, but I never thought there were people who walk cops."

He raised his flashlight, turned, and headed back.

Old Ding's apprentice said disapprovingly:

"Shifu, you'll do anything for a laugh."

Moving up close to his apprentice and keeping his voice low, he said:

"Little Hu, now I understand, it was a pair of spirits."

As soon as the words left his mouth, he felt a chill run up and down his spine and his scalp tighten; at the same time, however, he felt enormous relief. His apprentice, on the other hand, was even more disapproving:

"Shifu, you really will do anything for a laugh, won't you?"

Man and Beast

AS YET ANOTHER DAWN BROKE, A THICK, BILLOWING FOG BANK made its slow way across the Sapporo Sea toward land. First it filled the lush valleys, then it rose with a flourish to encircle the peak and the thick underbrush growing there. Crisp yet mysterious sounds from a clear mountain stream were released into the fog as it staggered down past the black cliffs to the valley below. Granddad lay on his stomach in a cave halfway up the mountain, where he had taken shelter, listening warily to the sounds of the surging spring, the crowing of roosters in the village as they heralded the dawn, and the deep rumble of the ocean tide.

I often imagine myself one day setting out to sea with a large sum of money earned through my own labor — once People's Currency has become strong in world markets — taking the route the Japanese used back then to transport Chinese conscript laborers. When I reach the island of Hokkaido, armed with the images of the route Granddad described for me hundreds of times as he told his story, I will search out the cave on a mountain facing the sea, the place where he took shelter for more than ten years.

*   *   *

The fog rose up to the mouth of the cave, where it merged with the underbrush and dense creeping vines to block Granddad's view. The walls of the dank cave were covered with copper-colored moss and lichens. Several supple animal furs were draped across stone outcroppings; the smell of fox emanated from the walls, a constant reminder of his heroism or his savagery in taking over the fox lair that was now his home. By then, Granddad had already forgotten just when it was that he'd fled to the mountain.

I have no way of knowing how someone who exists like a wolf for fourteen years in an ancient mountain forest views time or senses its passage. Maybe for him ten years went by like a single day, or maybe each day seemed to last ten years. His tongue had stiffened, but every syllable sounded clearly in his thoughts and in his ears: What a dense fog! A Japanese fog! And so the events of 1939, the fourteenth day of the eighth lunar month, when the troops under his command, including his son, hid beneath the Black Water River bridge to ambush a Japanese column of trucks, floated vividly into his mind. That too had been a morning when a great fog filled the sky.

Endless rows of red sorghum stalks rose up out of the dense fog. The roar of ocean waves crashing against rocks became the roar of truck engines. The crisp sound of a flowing stream trickling past stone became the sound of playful laughter from Douguan, my father. The patter of animal footsteps in the valley became the heavy breathing of Granddad and his troops.

The fog was heavy, like a flowing liquid, like the cotton candy spun by Liu the Second in the village of Saltwater Harbor. You could hold it in your hand, or reach out and tear off a piece. When my aunt Little Huaguan ate the cotton candy, it stuck to her mouth like a white beard. She was hoisted on the bayonet of a Jap devil. . . . A crippling pain made him curl into a ball. He bared his teeth and loosed a howl that rose from deep down in his throat. It was not the sound of a man, and, of course, it was not the sound of a wolf. It was the sound Granddad made in his fox lair.

Bullets raked the area, and the tips of sorghum stalks cascaded to the ground. Shells dragged long tails behind them as they tore through the fog. They flew into the fox cave, lighting up the stone walls like molten steel, beads of clear water sizzling on hot metal, sending the odor of steam into his nostrils. On one of the outcroppings hung strips of light brown fox fur. Water in the river, scalded by bullets, cried out like the screeching of birds. The red-feathered thrush, the green-feathered lark. White eels turned belly-up in the emerald waters of the Black Water River. Large dogfish with black skins and gritty flesh leaped with loud splashes in the valley stream. Douguan's hand shook as he aimed his Browning pistol. He fired! The black steel helmet was like the shell of a turtle. *Ping ping ping!* You lousy Jap!

I cannot actually witness the scene of Granddad lying in his cave thinking of his homeland, but I'll never forget a habit he brought home with him. No matter how comfortable the bed, he always slept on his stomach, knees bent, his chin pillowed on crossed arms. He was like a wild animal, always wary. We could never be sure when he was sleeping and when he was awake. But the first thing I saw each time I awoke were his bright green eyes. So I have a mental picture of how he slept in his cave and of the look on his face as he lay there.

His body stayed the same as always — that is, his bone structure didn't change. His muscles, however, twitched from the constant tension. Blood flowed powerfully through his tiny veins, building up strength, like a taut bowstring. The nose on his thin, oblong face was hard as iron, his eyes burned like charcoal fires. The tangled, iron-colored hair on his head looked like a raging prairie fire.

As the fog expanded it became thin, transparent, and buoyant. From within its wavering, crisscrossing, white silk bands emerged the tips of the underbrush, the creeping nets of vines, treetops in the forest, the rigid face of the village, and the ash blue teeth of the sea. The fiery red faces of sorghum stalks often shone through the fog. But as the fog thinned out, the frequency of sorghum faces lessened. The brutal Japanese landscape mercilessly filled the gaps in the fog, and forced out Granddad's dreams of his homeland. Eventually the haze retreated to the wooded valley.

The red glow of an enormous ocean filled Granddad's eyes. Ash blue waves licked lazily at the sandy beach, and a blood-red ball of fire burned its way out of the depths of the ocean.

Granddad could not recall, nor was there any way he could re-call, how many times he had watched the dripping wet sun leap out of the water. The blood-red fire of hope, so hot it made him tremble, raged in his heart. A vast stretch of sorghum formed neat ranks in the ocean. The stalks were the erect bodies of his sons and daughters, the leaves were their arms waving in the air, sabers glinting in the sunlight. The Japanese ocean became a sea of sorghum, the undulations of the ocean were the rising and falling chests of sorghum stalks, and the coursing tide was sorghum blood.

According to an entry in the historical records of Hokkaido's Sapporo city, Yoshikawa Sadako, a peasant woman from the nearby village of Kiyota, went out to a rice paddy in the valley on the morning of October 1, 1949, where she encountered a savage who violated her. A Japanese friend of mine, Mr. Nagano, helped me locate this material and translated it into Chinese for me. The so-called savage was my granddad, and my purpose in citing this material is to pin down the time and place in which an important event in my granddad's narrative occurred. In the Mid-Autumn Festival of 1943, he was cap-tured and later taken to Hokkaido as a conscript laborer. In the spring of 1944, when mountain flowers were in full bloom, he escaped from a labor camp and began his life in the mountains as part man and part beast. By October 1, 1949, the day the People's Republic was proclaimed, he had spent more than two thousand days and nights in the forest. Now the morning I'm describing, aside from the great fog that made it easy but more gut-wrenching for him to recall the fervent life he and his loved ones had led back home, has no particular significance. What happened later that afternoon is another story.

It was a typical Hokkaido morning. The fog had dispersed and the sun hung high above the sea and the forest. A few dazzling white sails drifted slowly on the water. From a distance they didn't seem to be moving at all. Strips of brown seaweed lay drying in the sun on the sand. Japanese fishermen gathering the seaweed wriggled in the shallow water, like so many large brown beetles. Ever since suffering at the hands of a gray-bearded fisherman, my granddad was filled with hatred for the Japanese, whether they wore cruel or kind faces. Now when he went down to the village at night to steal seaweed and dried fish, he no longer experienced the worthless sense of guilt. He went so far as to rip up the fishing nets drying on the beach with a pair of rusty old scissors.

The sun baked down. Even the wispy fog in the valley had dissipated, and the ocean was turning white. On trees all over the mountain, large red and yellow leaves mingled with the vibrant green of pine and cedar, like tongues of fire. Sprinkled amid the deep reds and greens were columns of pure white — the bark of birch trees. Another lovely autumn day had quietly arrived. After the autumn came the severe winters, those bitter Hokkaido winters, the kind that forced Granddad to hibernate like a bear. Generally speaking, there was more fat on his body when purple flowers that were the sign of autumn bloomed on the mountain. The prospects for this particular winter were good, mainly because three days earlier he had secured this cave: open to the sun, back to the wind, it was a good and safe place to hide. His next step was to store up food for the winter. He planned to go out on ten separate nights to bring back twenty partially dried bundles of seaweed. If his luck held out, he might also be able to steal a few dried fish or potatoes.

The stream was not far from his cave, which meant he wouldn't need to worry about leaving prints in the snow, since he climbed over vines and across creepers. This would be a good winter, thanks to the cave. It was his lucky day, and he was happy. Naturally, he could not know that on that day all China quivered with excitement. As he thought about his good prospects, his son — my father — was riding a mule, wearing a new army uniform, a rifle slung over his back. He and his unit had assembled under a locust tree at the foot of the Imperial City's eastern wall, where they waited to take part in the glorious parade at Tiananmen.

Sunlight filtered through leaves and branches into Granddad's cave and fell on his hands. His fingers were the color of metal, and gnarled like talons. Scaly flakes covered the backs of his hands, and his fingernails were chipped and broken. The backs of his hands were hot and itchy from the sun. Still somewhat sleepy, he closed his eyes, and as he dozed he heard the rumble of gunfire off in the distance. The competing brilliance of gold and red lights formed a column of a thousand fine steeds, like a brocade tapestry, like the rushing tide, streaming out from his chest. The intimate connection created between Granddad's hallucination and the joyous celebration of nation founding added splendor to Granddad's image. There are, of course, all sorts of theories — telepathy or supernatural powers — that might explain this inexplicable phenomenon.

Living on the mountain for years endowed Granddad with exceptionally keen senses of hearing and smell. This was not an unusual effect, nor was it a boastful fabrication; it was ıply an indisputable fact. Facts are superior to eloquence, and lies cannot cover up facts. That's what Granddad often said at public meetings. Inside his cave he pricked up his ears and caught a faint noise outside. The vines had moved slightly. It wasn't the wind. He knew the form and character of the wind, and could smell the difference in dozens of wind types. As he looked at the trembling vines he detected the smell of a fox, and he knew that retaliation had finally arrived. Ever since taking his knife to all four downy-furred fox cubs and tossing them out of the cave, Granddad had waited for the fox's retaliation. He was not afraid. He was fired up. After he had retreated from the world of men, the beasts had become his companions and his adversaries: wolves, bears, foxes. He knew them all well, and they knew him. After a bout of mortal combat with a bear, they had stayed out of each other's way. They still bared their teeth when they met, but their roars were intended as much to offer greetings as to display fierceness; neither would violate their gentleman's agreement of not attacking each other. The wolf feared my granddad; it was not a worthy adversary. When confronting a more ferocious animal, the wolf is no match for even a homeless mutt. But the fox, in contrast to the wolf and the bear, is a crafty, cunning little fellow, fierce only in the face of a wild hare or a farmhouse chicken.

He picked up his two prized possessions — a cleaver and a pair of scissors — one in each hand. The distinctive stink of fox and the rustling of the vines grew more acute. It was climbing toward him on the vines. Granddad had thought all along that this attack would happen in deep night. A fox's resourcefulness and liveliness is tied to the darkness of night. This broad daylight challenge to recover lost territory and avenge the murder of its cubs surprised him. When troops advance, a general mounts a defense; when floodwaters rise, there will be dirt to stop it. In other words, things will take care of themselves. Having faced far greater dangers many times, Granddad was calm and self-assured. Compared to most days, when all he did was lie low, this morning promised plenty of excitement. On the other side of the ocean, mighty mounted troops were at that moment parading past their heroic leader as he announced in a booming voice the creation of the People's Republic, while below, hundreds of thousands of faces were bathed in hot tears.

Clinging to a thick vine with its claws, the fiery red fox climbed to the level of the cave where Granddad was hiding. She wore a crafty smile and squinted in the bright sunlight. The circles around her eyes were jet black, and thick golden eyelashes sprang from her eyelids. It was the mother fox. Granddad saw two rows of dark teats, swollen with milk for the cubs she had lost. The large, fleshy red fox clung to the purple vine, her bushy tail sweeping alluringly back and forth, like a rogue melon, like an evil flame that can make even iron will waver.

Granddad felt a sudden weariness in the hand holding the cleaver. His fingers grew stiff, sore, and numb. The source of his problem lay in the fox's expression. She should have been baring her teeth in a savage snarl, instead of wagging her tail seductively and smiling sweetly. The sight stupefied Granddad and turned his fingers numb. The gently swaying vine was only a couple of feet away from the mouth of the cave. The fireball overhead shone down on the leaves of the underbrush,

SHIFU, YOU'LL DO ANYTHING FOR A LAUGH

transforming them into shards of gold foil. All he had to do was reach out and chop through the vine to send the fox plunging into the valley below, but he couldn't lift his hand. The enchantment of the fox was boundless, the heft of his cleaver immeasurable. Legends of foxes surged into his mind, and he wondered when he had amassed so much fox lore. With no pistol at hand, he felt his courage wane. Back in those days when he'd sat astride his black steed, weapon in hand, he had feared nothing.

High-pitched trills from the fox accompanied the wagging of her tail, imitating the sound of a weeping woman. Granddad couldn't understand why he hesitated, why he was suddenly impotent. Aren't you still the bandit Yu Zhan'ao, who killed without batting an eye? He clutched the crumbling handle of his knife and hunkered down to await the attack from the fox as it swung back and forth on the vine. His heart was thumping, and spurts of icy blood rushed to his skull, suffusing the area in front of his eyes with the color of ice and water. Prickly pains attacked his temples. Apparently, the fox had seen through his plan of action. She was still swinging, but the arc was lessening. Now Granddad would have to lean way out to hack at her. The look on her face was more and more that of a lustful woman. It was a look with which he was very familiar. Granddad sensed that in an instant the fox could transform herself into a woman in white mourning clothes. So he thrust himself forward, grabbed the vine with one hand, and with the other aimed at the fox's head.

The fox swooped down. Granddad lunged after it, and nearly fell out of the cave. But he managed to strike the fox on the head with his rusty knife. Then, just as he was drawing his

68

body back into the cave, he heard a scream above him. A hot, fetid smell descended with the scream, enveloping his body. A large fox bore down on his back, its paws wrapped tightly around his chest and abdomen, its taut, bushy tail fanning the air excitedly. The coarse fur pricked painfully into Granddad's thighs. At the same time he felt the fox's hot breath on his neck, which hunched inward by reflex. Goose bumps covered his legs, as something dug excruciatingly into the nape of his neck. The fox was biting him. Only then did he comprehend the treachery of foxes in Hokkaido, Japan.

It was now impossible for him to retreat back into his cave. Even if he somehow managed to fight his way back in, the fox he'd injured slightly could climb in after him, and then the male and the female would attack, one in front, one in back, and Granddad would be a dead Granddad. He analyzed the situation with lightning speed. If he was willing to risk his life, there was a slim chance he'd survive. The male fox's razor-sharp teeth tore into him, and he could feel them touching bone. Crouching down quickly and letting the pitted cleaver and scissors fall to the valley floor, he grabbed a vine with both hands and, with the male fox clinging to his back, swung out and hung in the air.

Bright red beads of blood oozed from the wounds on the female fox's head. This Granddad saw as he leaped out of the cave. Hot blood from his neck ran onto his shoulders and flowed down to his abdomen and buttocks. The fox's teeth seem to be embedded in the fissures of his bones. Bone pain is seven or eight times worse than pain in the muscles; that was a conclusion he'd drawn from his experiences in China. And the teeth of a live animal are more terrible than shrapnel. The pain unleashed by the former is filled with the vibrancy of life; that of the latter is heavy with death. Granddad had hoped to rely on this death-defying leap to fling the male fox off his back, but its unyielding claws shattered those hopes. Like magnets or barbed hooks, they clung to Granddad's shoulders and waist. Its mouth and teeth had fused with his neck. The injured mother fox made things even more difficult for him, since she was not hurt badly enough to fall off the vine. Climbing forward another half meter or so to focus her attack, she bit into his foot. Even though the soles of his feet were so hard and calloused they were not bothered by brambles or thorns, he was, after all, only human, flesh and blood, and her sharp teeth were too much for him. He howled in pain as tears of agony clouded his vision.

Granddad shook himself hard. The foxes shook with him, but their teeth remained clamped into his flesh; if anything, they dug in even deeper. Let go, Granddad! Falling would be better than living like this. But he held the vine in a death grip. Never, in the long life of that vine, had it withstood such force. It creaked and twisted, as if groaning. Its roots were on the gentle slope of the mountain above the cave, where purple flowers were in full bloom amid red and yellow leaves that had fallen from high above. It was there that Granddad had discovered the crisp, sweet, juicy mountain radishes, which he'd added to his menu. It was also there that he'd discovered the serpentine fox path, which he'd followed — using vines to get to the melons — all the way to the foxes' lair, where he'd killed the cubs and flung them out of the cave. Granddad, if you'd known that you'd be suspended in the air, racked with pain, you wouldn't have killed those cubs and taken over the cave, would you? His ashen face was the color of steel. He said nothing.

The vine swung back and forth, sending dirt from above the cave raining down. The sun shone brightly, making the stream on the west side of the cave glisten as it snaked down to the trees in the valley. The village beyond the valley twirled on the beach, on which tens of thousands of ocean waves shimmered and broke, one rolling hard behind the other, never resting. The music of the ocean filtered into Granddad's ears, ten thousand galloping horses one minute, light dancing melodies the next. He clutched his vine tightly, determined not to let go.

The vines sent warnings to man and fox alike; man and fox kept twisting them about. They began to snap angrily. The mouth of the cave slowly rose in the air. Granddad held on for dear life. The precipice moved upward, as the lush, green valley rushed up to meet him. The cool, refreshing air of the forest and the smell of rotting leaves formed a soft cushion that cradled Granddad's belly. The long purple vines danced in the air. He could feel, he could sense, that the fox at his feet had broken loose from her vine, and as she fell she turned a graceful somersault, like a heavenly fire. Ocean waves tumbled onto the beach, curving like a horse's mane.

As he fell, Granddad had no thoughts of dying. He said that after his rope had broken in three attempts at suicide in the forest one year, he knew he would not die. He had a premonition that his final resting place would be back in Northeast Gaomi Township, on the other side of the ocean. And since he'd rid himself of the fear of death, falling became a rare opportunity to experience joy. His body seemed to flatten out, his consciousness turning transparently thin. His heart stopped beating, his blood ceased its flow, and the pit of his stomach was slightly red and warm, like a charcoal brazier. Granddad sensed the wind peeling the male fox away from him — first its legs, then its mouth. That mouth seemed to have taken away something from his neck, but it seemed to have left something as well. His burden was abruptly lifted, and Granddad smoothly turned three hundred and sixty degrees in the air. That revolution gave him a chance to look at the male fox and at its pointy, savage face. Its fur was greenish yellow, except for the belly, which was white as snow. Naturally, he could see that it would make a fine pelt, something he could make into a leather vest. The treetops rose faster and faster — pagoda-shaped snow pines, birches with white bark, and oaks with yellow leaves fluttering like butterflies. He tumbled into their outstretched canopies.

Granddad was still holding on to the spiraling vine for dear life when it caught on a strong but yielding limb of an oak tree. As he hung in the canopy of the tree, he heard the crack of branches snapping. He fell into the crotch of a thick limb and sprang up into the air; again he hit the limb and again he bounced into the air. Finally he came to rest under the vibrating tree, just in time to see the two foxes, first one and then the other, as they thudded into the thick carpet of dead leaves. Like a pair of explosives, the two soft bodies sent rank mud and rotting leaves flying off in all directions. Two dull thuds rustled the dead leaves, the older ones fluttering down to blanket a pair of similarly dead foxes. Gazing down at the brilliantly colored foxes as they were being buried by red and yellow leaves, Granddad suddenly felt his chest expand with heat. A sweet taste filled his mouth, and a red flag slowly unfurled in his skull. Lights went on all around him, and his pain vanished into thin air. His heart overflowed with warm sentiments toward the foxes. The image of them descending gracefully into a bed of red and yellow leaves flowed in and out of his mind. Curtly I said, Granddad, you passed out.

The call of a bird awakened Granddad. The scorching noonday sun baked parts of his skin, streams of glorious golden light filtering through gaps between branches and leaves. Light green squirrels leaped nimbly about the tree as they plucked acorns and gnawed at the husks, exposing the white flesh underneath with its subtle bitter aroma. Granddad began to grow aware of his body. His internal organs were all right; his legs were all right. His foot ached, and there were black clots of blood and torn flesh where the female fox had bitten. His neck hurt where the male fox had buried his teeth. Unsure of where his arms were, he searched for them and found them raised high over his head, still grasping the vine that had saved his life. Experience told him that they were dislocated. He straightened up. Dizzy, he stopped looking down. Using his teeth, he pried his fingers off the vine. Then, with his legs and the tree trunk for support, he worked his arms back into their sockets. He heard the pop of bone and felt sweat ooze from his pores. A woodpecker was attacking a tree nearby. The pain in his neck returned with a vengeance, as if the woodpecker's pointy beak were tapping on one of his white nerves. The cries of birds in the forest could not drown out the sound of ocean waves, and he knew that the ocean was very close. The moment he lowered his head he felt dizzy, and that was the greatest peril in climbing down from the tree. But it would be suicide to stay where he was. His guts were tied in knots, his throat was parched.

Straining to get his nearly useless arms working, he put his legs and belly to work as he began his descent from the tree, forcing his body hard against the trunk. But his efforts were not rewarded, as he tumbled headlong down to the ground. The carpet of rotting leaves cushioned his fall. He'd fallen too short a distance to cause an explosion. The sweet, acrid stench rising up from under him overwhelmed his sense of smell. He got to his feet and, with the sound of water in his ears, began to stumble forward. The stream was hidden beneath the rotting leaves, and as his foot stepped down on them, a coolness rose toward him, and water seeped up from where he had stepped. He lay on his belly and parted the rotting leaves, layer after layer, where the sound of the water was the loudest. It was like peeling away the layers of a flat cake. At first the water was murky; he waited a moment until it cleared. Then he lowered his head to drink, and the cold water rushed past his chest into his stomach; the fetid taste didn't come until later. That brought to my mind the moment during the war when he had lapped up the hot, dirty, tadpole-infested water of the Black Water River.

Once Granddad had drunk his fill, he felt much better and more energetic. All that water staved off his hunger for the time being. He reached up to feel the wound on his neck. It was a pulpy mess, and he recalled the stabbing pain when the fox's teeth snapped off as the animal was ripped away. Gritting his teeth, he probed the wound with his finger. As expected, he found a pair of fangs. Removing them started the flow of blood again, but not much, and he let it flow long enough to cleanse the wound. Then he held his breath and cleared his mind. From the powerful current of myriad forest smells, he picked out the unique, pungent scent of red-leafed loosestrife, and followed it to a spot behind a tall pine tree. I have never found reference to this plant in any illustrated encyclopedia of Chinese herbs. Granddad picked some of the herb and chewed it into a paste, which he rubbed on his wounds, one on his neck and another on his foot. To treat his dizziness, he went looking for purple-stalked peppermint. After tearing off a couple of leaves, he kneaded them until juice came out, then stuck them on his temples. Now his wounds no longer hurt. Beneath a chestnut oak tree he ate a few clusters of nonpoisonous mushrooms, and followed that with some sweet mountain leeks. He was in luck, for he also discovered some wild grapes. Once he'd satisfied his hunger, he emptied his bowels and bladder. He had now turned himself back into an energized mountain spirit.

He walked over to look at the foxes beneath an oak tree. Bottleneck flies were already swarming over them. Always afraid of flies, he backed off. Sap flowing from a pine tree gave off a fragrant odor. Bears were sleeping inside the hollows of trees; wolves were nursing their strength in rocky lairs. Granddad knew that he should return to his mountain cave, but he was drawn to the comforting sound of ocean waves and defied his own pattern of staying hidden in the day and going out only at night. Boldly — he was never afraid — he walked toward the sound of the waves.

The ocean sounded very near, but was actually some distance away. Granddad passed through the forest, as long and narrow as the valley, and climbed a gently sloping ridge where the trees gradually began to thin out. The ground was dotted with stumps of felled trees. He knew this ridge well, even though until today he had only seen it at night. The colors were different, and so were the smells. Amid the wooded areas were spots where anemic stalks of corn and mung beans had been planted. Granddad squatted down between two rows and ate a few green mung beans, which left a grainy residue on his tongue. He felt serene and unhurried, like a peasant with no concerns. It was a mood he'd experienced only a few times during his fourteen years on the mountain. The time he'd extracted salt from the inlet with his aluminum teapot was one of those. The time he'd stuffed himself with potatoes was another. Each had been a special situation, memorable in its own way.

After eating the mung beans, he walked the last few hundred meters to the top of the ridge, where he looked at the blue waters of the ocean that had drawn him to this spot and at the gray village below the ridge. The seaside was quiet; an old-looking man was turning over the strips of seaweed that lay drying in the sun. The village began to stir, starting with the sound of cattle cries. This was the first time he'd approached the village in the light of day, and he had an unobstructed view of what a Japanese village really looked like. Aside from the unusual style of the buildings, it was strikingly similar to farming villages in Northeast Gaomi Township. The odd bark of a sick, feeble dog warned him that he mustn't brave going any closer. If he were spotted in the daylight, escape would be difficult, if not impossible. So he hid behind some brambles and watched the village and the ocean for a while. Growing bored, he headed back in a relaxed mood. But then he was reminded of the cleaver and scissors he'd lost in the valley, and panic set in. Without those little treasures, just getting by would be nearly impossible. He quickened his step.

On the ridge he saw a cornfield where the stalks were rustling in wind that sounded very near. He squatted down and hid behind a tree. The field was no larger than a few acres, and the thin, stumpy ears of corn did not look healthy, apparently deprived of both fertilizer and water. Drifting back in time, he detected the smell of burning mugwort. Mosquitoes were buzzing around the edges of the smoke; a cricket in a pear tree chirped shrilly; in the darkness a horse was eating bran mixed with hay; an owl in a graveyard cypress hooted sorrowfully; and the deep, thick night was drenched with dew. Someone coughed in the cornfield. It was a woman. Granddad was startled out of his reveries, excited and afraid.

People were what he feared the most, and also what he missed the most.

In the grip of excitement and fear, he held his breath and focused his eyes, wanting to have a look at the woman in the cornfield. She'd only coughed once, lightly, but he could tell it was a woman. His hearing sharpened and he smelled the scent of a Japanese woman.

She finally appeared in the cornfield. Her face was ashen, her large, single-fold eyes gloomy. She had a thin nose and a small, delicate mouth. Granddad felt no malice toward her. She removed her tattered scarf to reveal uncombed brown hair. She was obviously undernourished, just like starving women in China. Granddad's fear was quietly replaced by a sort of pity wholly inappropriate to the situation. She set a basket of corn on the ground and wiped her sweaty brow with her scarf, streaking her ashen face.

She wore a loose, bulky, badly faded yellow jacket, which gave rise to wicked thoughts in Granddad. Thin autumn breezes blew. From the forest came the monotonous tapping of a woodpecker. Behind him the ocean was panting. Granddad heard her mutter something in a low, hoarse voice. Like most Japanese women, her neck and chest were white. Brazenly, she unbuttoned her clothing to allow in the breeze, observed fixedly by Granddad. He saw from her swollen breasts that she was a nursing mother. When Douguan squirmed as he hung at Grandma's breast, she had spanked his round bottom. Now the spare, stalwart Douguan was sitting high on the back of his steed, holding the reins loosely as he galloped past Tiananmen Gate. The clatter of the horse's iron shoes rang out on the stone-paved avenue, as he and his companions shouted slogans that rocked heaven and earth. He wanted to turn to look at the men standing atop the wall, but strict discipline kept him from doing so. All he could do was catch a glimpse of the great men standing beneath the red lanterns out of the corner of his eye.

She had no reason to cover herself on that bleak, deserted mountain ridge as she urinated. The entire process was aimed straight at Granddad, who felt his blood surge; his wounds throbbed painfully. He stood up in a crouch, mindless of the noise his arms made as they bumped into branches of the tree.

The woman's lackluster gaze suddenly focused, and Granddad watched her mouth open wide. A cry of apparent terror tore from her mouth. Off balance, yet with lightning speed, Granddad rushed toward the woman. How frightening he must have looked.

Not long afterward, he would see his reflection in the clear water of the stream, and realize why the Japanese woman had crumpled like a rag doll there in the cornfield.

Granddad laid her down, her body yielding to his positioning. Ripping open her blouse, he saw her heart pounding wildly beneath her breasts. The woman was skin and bones, her body sticky with sweat and filth.

Granddad tore at her, spewing words of foul revenge, one string after another, echoing in his ears: Japan! Little Japanese! Jap bastards! You raped and killed my women, bayoneted my daughter, enslaved my people, slaughtered my troops, trampled on my countrymen, and burned down our houses. The blood debt between us is as great as the ocean. Ha ha. Today your woman has fallen into my hands!

Hatred turned his eyes blood red. His teeth itched. An evil flame hardened him like steel. He slapped her. He tore at her hair and squeezed her breasts. He dug his fingers into her flesh. She trembled and moaned, as if talking in her sleep.

Granddad's voice continued to roar in his ears, spewing filth: Why don't you fight? I'm going to rape you, kill you! I'm going to fuck you to death! An eye for an eye! Are you dead? Even if you are, I won't let go of you!

He ripped off her lower garments, the tattered cloth tearing easily, like cardboard. Granddad told me that when her lower garments fell, the hot blood that had been surging through his body abruptly turned cold, and his body, hard as rifle steel, suddenly went limp, like a rooster that's lost a cockfight, hanging its head in defeat, its feathers torn and ragged.

Granddad said he saw a black patch sewn in the crotch of her red underwear, and lost heart.

Granddad, how could a hardened son of China like you be afraid of a patch? Did it violate some taboo of your Iron Society?

My grandson, it wasn't a patch that your granddad feared!

Granddad said that seeing the black patch on the crotch of the woman's red underpants was like being hit in the head with a club.

The Japanese woman became an icy corpse. The field of fiery red sorghum from twenty-five years earlier once again surged before him, like a galloping horse. It muddled his vision and flooded his mind. Desolate music resounded deep in his soul, each note a hammer pounding against his heart, and in that sea of blood, in that fiery oven, on that holy sacrificial altar, was Grandma, laid out face-up like a lovely piece of jade, the body of a sweet young girl. Her clothing too had been ripped open to expose the same sort of red underwear, with a similar black patch over the crotch. That time Granddad had not turned limp and weak, and that black patch had become a symbol that was burned into his memory, never to disappear. His tears flowed down to the corners of his mouth, where he tasted a mixture of sweetness and bitterness.

Granddad roughly straightened the woman's clothes with his weary hands. The bruises on her body brought him deep remorse. Staggering to his feet, he started to walk away. His legs were sore and numb. The hot, swollen wound on his neck throbbed, as if engorged with pus. The trees and the mountain peak before him were transformed into a dazzling crimson. Way up high, in the upper reaches of heaven, there in the

clouds, Grandma, her chest riddled with bullets, fell slo\
into Granddad's outstretched arms. When all her blood h⌐ɹ
flowed out, her body became as light as a beautiful red butterfly. Cupping her in his hands, he walked ahead, down a path
opened amid the supple stalks of sorghum. Light from the
path streaked skyward; light from the heavens streamed down,
fusing heaven and earth. He was standing on the tall embankment of the Black Water River, where yellow weeds grew and
white flowers bloomed. The water, the brilliant color of blood,
congealed into oil, so bright it was a mirror that reflected the
blue sky and white clouds, the dove and the goshawk. Granddad fell headlong into the cornfield on the Japanese mountain
ridge; it was like falling into a sorghum field in his homeland.

Granddad never actually had intercourse with that woman,
so the furry baby described in Japanese historical materials,
the one she eventually bore, is not related to him. But even
having a young uncle who is half Japanese and has a body covered with hair would be no disgrace to our family, and could, in
fact, be considered our glory. One must honor the truth.

Soaring

AFTER PAYING RESPECTS TO HEAVEN AND EARTH, HONG XI, A BIG, swarthy man, could not contain his excitement. His bride's veiled face was hidden from him, but her long, shapely arms and willowy waist revealed that she was more beautiful than most girls in Northern Jiaozhou Township. Forty years old, and badly pockmarked, Hong Xi was one of Northeast Gaomi Township's most prominent bachelors. His aging mother had recently arranged for him to marry Yanyan in exchange for his sister, Yanghua, one of Northeast Gaomi's true beauties, who was to marry Yanyan's elder brother, a mute. Deeply touched by his sister's sacrifice, Hong Xi thought about her bearing children for the mute, and amid his confused emotions was born a hostility toward his new bride. Mute, if you mess up my little sister, I'll take it out on yours.

It was noon when Hong Xi's new wife entered the bridal chamber. A cluster of prankish children had poked holes in the pink paper window covering to gawk at the bride as she sat on the edge of the brick bed. A neighbor woman patted Hong Xi on the shoulder and giggled, "Pocky, you're a lucky man! That's a tender little lotus bud you've got, so handle it gently."

Hong Xi fidgeted with his trousers and snickered. The marks on his face glowed red.

The sun hung motionless in the sky, as Hong Xi paced back and forth in the yard, waiting for night to fall. His mother hobbled up with her cane and said, "Xi, there's something about my new daughter-in-law that bothers me. Be careful she doesn't run off."

"Don't worry, Mother. With Yanghua over there, this one's not going anywhere. They're like locusts tied together with a string. One can't get away without the other."

While mother and son were talking, the new daughter-in-law walked out into the yard accompanied by two bridesmaids. Hong Xi's mother muttered disapprovingly, "Whoever heard of a bride getting up off the bed before dark to relieve herself? That just shows the marriage won't last. I think she's up to something."

But Hong Xi was too taken with his wife's beauty to share his mother's concern. She had a long face, fine eyebrows, a high nose, and slanted eyes like those of a phoenix. But when she spotted Hong Xi's face, she stopped in her tracks and, after a long quiet moment, let out a screech and took off running. The bridesmaids reached out to grab her by the arms, and *rip*, tore her red gown to reveal the snowy white skin of her arms, her slender neck, and the front of the red camisole she wore underneath.

Hong Xi was stunned. Rapping him on the head with her cane, his mother shouted, "Go after her, you fool!"

That snapped him out of it, and he staggered after her.

Yanyan flew down the street, trailing her loosened hair like the tail of a bird.

"Stop her!" Hong Xi shouted. "Stop her!"

His shouts brought villagers swarming out of their houses into the street and drew frantic barks from a dozen or more big, ferocious dogs.

Yanyan turned down a lane and headed south into the field, where wheat stalks bent in the wind, their flowered tips dipping like waves in an ocean of green. Yanyan crashed through the waist-high waves of wheat, their green contrasting with her red camisole and milky white arms, a lovely painting in motion.

A bride fleeing from her wedding disgraced all of Northeast Gaomi Township. So the village men took up the chase with a vengeance, coming at her from all sides. The dogs, too, which leaped and bounded in the waves of green.

As the human net closed in, Yanyan dove headfirst into the waves of wheat.

Hong Xi breathed a sigh of relief. The pursuers slowed down, breathing heavily; grasping hands, they moved with great care, like fishermen tightening a net.

As anger gripped his heart, all Hong Xi could think about was the beating he'd give her once she was in his grasp.

All of a sudden, a beam of red light rose above the wheat field, startling and confusing the mob below, who fell to the ground. Then they spotted Yanyan, her hands flapping in the air, her legs held together like a gorgeous butterfly, as she rose gracefully out of the encirclement.

The people froze like clay statues, gaping as she flapped her arms and hovered above them, then began to fly, slowly enough for them to keep stepping on her shadow if they ran after her. She was only six or seven meters above their heads, but, oh, so graceful, so lovely. Just about every oddity you could think of had occurred in Northeast Gaomi Township, but this was the first time a woman had taken to the sky.

Once the shock had passed, the people recommenced their pursuit. Some ran home and returned on bicycles to take up the chase of her shadow, waiting for her to land so they could grab her.

The flyer and the people below acted out an engrossing drama of pursuit and capture amid the shouts of people all across the fields. Out-of-towners joined passersby in craning their necks to watch the strange event in the sky. The woman in flight was mesmerizingly graceful; her pursuers below, always having to look up as they ran, stumbled through the rutted fields, falling and crashing into one another like a routed army.

Eventually, Yanyan settled into a grove of pine trees surrounding the old graveyard on the eastern edge of town. The black pines, covering nearly an acre, kept watch over hundreds of mounds under which Northeastern Gaomi ancestors lay. The trees, all very old, stood straight and tall, their tips piercing the low-flying clouds. Together, the old graveyard and the grove of black pines were the township's scariest and most sacred spot. Sacred because it was the resting place of the township's ancestors; scariest owing to all the ghostly incidents that had occurred there.

Yanyan settled onto the tip of the tallest and oldest pine tree, in the very center of the graveyard. The people below followed her there, then stood and looked up to where she rested lightly on the slender topmost branches of the tree, which easily supported her, even though she must have weighed over a hundred pounds; it was a cause of wonderment to all who were gazing from below.

A dozen or more dogs raised their heads and bayed at the levitating Yanyan.

Hong Xi shouted, "Come down, come down from there this minute."

The dogs' baying and Hong Xi's shouts fell on deaf ears. Yanyan sat there nonchalantly, rising and falling with each passing breeze.

The crowd below soon grew weary of standing there helplessly, except for a few rambunctious kids, who shouted, "New bride, hey there, new bride, let's see you fly some more!"

Yanyan raised her arms. Fly, the kids shouted, fly, she's going to fly. But she didn't. Instead, she combed her talonlike fingers through her hair, like a bird preening its feathers.

Hong Xi fell to his knees and wailed, "Uncles, brothers, fellow townspeople, help me find a way to bring her down. You know how hard it was for me to find a wife!"

Just then Hong Xi's mother was led up on a donkey. She slid down off the animal's back, groaning in pain as she stumbled to the ground.

"Where is she?" the old woman asked Hong Xi. "Where is she?"

Hong Xi pointed to the treetop. "She's up there."

Screening her eyes with her hand, the old woman looked up to where her daughter-in-law was nestled atop the tree and screamed, "Demon, she's a demon!"

Iron Mountain, the township head, said, "We have to find a way to get her down, demon or not. This has to come to an end, like everything else."

"Elder," the old woman said, "please take charge of this, I beg you."

To which Iron Mountain replied, "Here's what we'll do. First, we send someone to Northern Jiaozhou Township to fetch her mother, her brother, and Yanghua. Then if she won't come down, we keep Yanghua here and not let her go back. Next, we send some people home to make bows and arrows and cut some long poles. If nothing else works, we'll bring her down the hard way. And we'll report this to the local government. Since she and Hong Xi are man and wife, the government will surely step in to uphold the marriage laws. Right, then. Hong Xi, you keep watch here under the tree. We'll send someone back with a gong. If anything happens, bang it for all you're worth. The way she's acting, I'm pretty sure she's possessed. We'll have to go back to town and kill a dog so we can have some dog blood at hand when we need it."

The crowd broke up and headed back to make preparations. Hong Xi's mother insisted upon staying with her son, but Iron Mountain was adamant. "Don't be silly. What can you hope to accomplish by staying here? If the situation turns ugly, you'll be caught in the middle. Go on home." Seeing it was pointless to argue, the old woman let herself be boosted up on the donkey's back and left the scene weeping and wailing.

Now that the tumult had died down, Hong Xi, who was known as one of Northeast Gaomi Township's bravest souls, found the quiet unsettling. As the sun set in the west, winds swirled and moaned amid the trees. Letting his head droop, Hong Xi massaged his sore neck and sat down on a nearby stone tablet. He was lighting a cigarette when a sinister laugh floated down from above. His hair stood on end, and he felt chilled all over. Quickly extinguishing the match, he stood up and backed off several steps to look up at the treetop. "Don't pull any spooky tricks on me. Just wait till I get my hands on you."

With the setting sun as a backdrop, Yanyan's red camisole seemed to be on fire, setting her face aglow, as if gilded. There was no sign that the sinister laughter had come from her. A flock of crows returning to their nests flew past, their gray droppings falling like rain. Several warm blobs landed squarely on his head. Spitting on the ground, he felt that bad luck had befallen him. The treetop was still radiant with light, even though the pine grove was turning black and bats had begun flitting nimbly in and among the trees. Foxes barked in the graveyard. His fears returned.

Spirits were everywhere in the grove, he could feel them; his ears filled with all sorts of sounds. The sinister laughter kept coming, each burst causing him to break out in a cold sweat. Biting the tip of your middle finger was the best way to drive away evil spirits, he recalled, so he did it, and the sharp pain cleared his head. Now he could see that the pine grove wasn't as dark as it had seemed just a moment before. Rows of grave mounds and headstones stood out. He could make out the tree trunks, streaked with dying rays of sunlight. Some young foxes were frolicking amid the grave mounds, watched over by their mother as she crouched in a clump of weeds, every so often acknowledging his presence with a toothy grin. The next time he looked skyward, he saw Yanyan, who hadn't moved, being circled by the crows.

A pale little boy emerged from between two trees, handed

him a gong and a mallet, a hatchet, and a large flat cake. The boy told him that Iron Mountain was overseeing the making of bows and arrows, that people had been sent to Northern Jiaozhou, and that the township leaders were taking the incident very seriously; they would be sending someone over soon. Hong Xi was to satisfy his hunger with the flat cake and maintain his vigil. He should beat the gong if anything happened.

Once the little boy had left, Hong Xi laid the gong on the memorial stone, shoved the hatchet into his belt, and began devouring the flat cake. As soon as he was finished, he took out the hatchet and shouted, "Are you going to come down or not? If not, I'll chop down this tree."

Not a sound from Yanyan.

So Hong Xi buried his hatchet in the tree, which shuddered from the force. Still no sound from Yanyan. The hatchet was buried so deeply he couldn't pull it out.

Is she dead? Hong Xi wondered.

Tightening his belt and removing his shoes, Hong Xi began to climb. The rough bark made for easy going, and when he'd climbed about halfway, he stopped to look up. All he could see from that vantage point were her legs hanging down and her buttocks resting on the branch. We should be in bed together by now, he thought angrily, but instead you've got me climbing a tree. His anger was translated into strength, and as the trunk narrowed, more and more limbs branched off, making it easy to hoist himself up into the canopy, where he anchored his feet and reached out furtively to grab her. But no sooner had he touched the tip of her foot than he heard a long sigh and felt the branches above him rustle; flecks of gold flew into the air, like the golden scales of a leaping carp. Yanyan flapped her arms and lifted off from the canopy; then, with all four limbs in motion and her hair floating in midair, she glided to the top of another tree. Hong Xi was alarmed to note that her flying skills had obviously improved since the wheat field.

She sat atop the new tree in the same posture as the first. Facing the rosy sunset, she presented a sight as moving as a new rose bloom. "Yanyan," Hong Xi called out tearfully, "my dear wife, come home and make a life with me. If you don't, I won't let Yanghua go to the bed of your mute brother —"

His shout still hung in the air when he heard a frightful crack beneath him, as the branch snapped and sent him crashing to the ground like a hunk of meat. He lay there for a long while before getting to his feet by propping himself up on the carpet of decaying pine needles and taking a couple of tentative steps by leaning on the trunk. Except for the expected aches and pains, he seemed intact — no broken bones. He searched the sky for Yanyan and all he saw was the moon, which sent watery rays filtering down through the pine branches to fall on a part of a grave mound here, the corner of a headstone there, and an occasional clump of moss. Yanyan was bathed in moonlight, a big, beautiful bird perched for the night on the top of a tree.

Someone beyond the pine grove called his name. He shouted back. Remembering the gong on the memorial stone, he picked it up, but couldn't find the mallet anywhere.

A noisy mob entered the pine grove with lanterns and torches and flashlights, casting their light in the spaces between trees and pushing back the moon's rays.

Among them were Yanyan's aging mother, her mute elder brother, and his sister, Yanghua. He also saw Iron Mountain and seven or eight able-bodied men from town, with bows and arrows slung over their back. Others came equipped with long poles, or hunting rifles, even bird nets. A handsome young man in an olive-drab uniform cinched at the waist with a wide leather belt was holding a service revolver. Hong Xi recognized him as a local policeman.

Noting the bruises and welts on Hong Xi's face, Iron Mountain asked, "How did that happen?"

"It's nothing," he said.

"Where is she?" Yanyan's mother asked loudly.

Someone aimed a flashlight at the tip of a tree, shining it directly on her face. The people heard the top branches rustle, then watched as a dark shadow slipped silently from that tree to the top of another.

"You bastards!" Yanyan's mother cursed. "I know you've killed my daughter and made up a story to trick this old widow and her orphaned son. How could a girl fly like an owl?"

"Calm down, Auntie," Iron Mountain said. "We wouldn't have believed it if we hadn't seen it with our own eyes. Let me ask you, did your daughter ever study under a master? Learn any unusual skills? Associate with witches? Sorcerers?"

"My daughter has never studied under any master," Yanyan's mother said, "or learned any unusual skills. And she certainly hasn't associated with witches or sorcerers. I never let her out of my sight when she was growing up, and she did as she was told. The neighbors all said what a nice girl I had. And now this nice girl spends one day in your house and turns into an eagle on a treetop. How did that happen? I won't rest till I find out what you did to her. Give me back my Yanyan or you'll never get Yanghua back again!"

"That's enough bickering, old auntie," the policeman said. "Keep your eyes on the treetop." He aimed his flashlight at the shadow atop the tree, then snapped it on, training its beam of light on Yanyan's face. With a flap of her arms, she rose into the air and glided to the top of yet another tree.

"Did you see her, old auntie?" the policeman asked.

"Yes," Yanyan's mother said.

"Is it your daughter?"

"It's my daughter."

"We don't want to take drastic measures unless we have to," the policeman said. "She'll listen to you if you tell her to come down from there."

Just then, Yanyan's mute brother began grunting excitedly and flapping his arms, as if mimicking his sister's flying motions.

Yanyan's mother was in tears. "What did I do in a previous life to bring this down on my head?"

"Try not to cry, old auntie," the policeman said. "Concentrate on getting your daughter down from there."

"She's always been a strong-willed girl. She might not listen to me," Yanyan's mother admitted sadly.

"This is no time to be shy, old auntie," the policeman said. "Call her down."

With mincing steps on tiny, bound feet, Yanyan's mother moved over to the tree where her daughter was perched, tilted her head back, and called out tearfully, "Yanyan, be a good girl and listen to your mother. Please come down. . . . I know you feel you've been treated badly, but that can't be helped. If you don't come down, we won't be able to keep Yanghua, and if that happens, the family's finished. . . ."

The old lady broke down and wailed at this point as she dashed her head against the tree trunk. A scratchy sound descended from the treetop, the sort of thing one hears when a bird ruffles its feathers.

"Keep talking," the policeman urged.

The mute waved his arms and grunted loudly to his sister, high above him.

"Yanyan," Hong Xi shouted, "you're still human, aren't you? If there's an ounce of humanity left in you, you'll come down from there."

Yanghua joined in the weeping: "Sister-in-law, please come down. You and I are both sufferers in this world. My brother's ugly, but at least he can talk. But your brother . . . please come down . . . it's our fate. . . ."

Yanyan glided into the air again and circled the sky above the people. Chilled dewdrops fell to the ground — maybe they were her tears.

"Move out of the way, give her some space and let her settle to the ground," Iron Mountain said to the crowd.

Everyone but the old lady and Yanghua stepped backwards.

But things did not turn out as Iron Mountain had hoped, for after circling in the air above them, Yanyan settled back down onto the treetop.

The moon had slipped into the western sky; the night was deepening. Fatigue and cold began to overtake the people on the ground. "I guess we'll have to do it the hard way," the policeman said.

Iron Mountain said, "I'm worried that the crowd might drive her away from the grove, and if we don't catch her tonight, it'll be that much harder later on."

"As I see it," the policeman said, "she lacks the ability to fly long distances, which means it'll actually be easier to catch her if she leaves the grove."

"But what if her family won't go along with our plan?" Iron Mountain said.

"Let me handle it," the policeman assured him.

He went over and told some of the youngsters to escort the mute and his mother out of the pine grove. The old lady, having cried herself into a state of lethargy, offered no resistance. The mute, on the other hand, grunted his disapproval, but once the policeman flashed his service revolver, he walked off meekly. Now the only people left at the scene were the policeman, Iron Mountain, Hong Xi, and two young men, one with a pole, the other holding a net.

"A gunshot might alarm the people," the policeman said. "So let's use a bow and arrow."

"With my failing eyesight," Iron Mountain said, "I'm not the one to do it. If my aim was off even a little, I could kill her. Hong Xi should do it."

He handed the bamboo bow and a feathered, razor-sharp arrow to Hong Xi, who took them from him, but merely stood there deep in thought. "I can't do it," he said, suddenly realizing what was expected of him. "I can't, I won't. She's my wife, isn't she? My wife."

"Hong Xi," Iron Mountain said, "don't be a fool! In your arms, she's your wife, but perched atop a tree, she's some kind of strange bird."

"You people," the policeman said with annoyance, "can't you do anything? If you're just going to stand there hemming and hawing, hand me that bow and arrow."

He holstered his revolver, took the bow and arrow, took aim at the shape at the top of the tree, and let an arrow fly. A muted thud told them he'd hit the mark. The treetop rustled, and the men watched as Yanyan, an arrow embedded in her belly, rose into the moonlight, only to crash into the canopy of a short tree nearby. Obviously, she could no longer keep her balance. The policeman fitted another arrow to the bow, took aim at Yanyan, who was sprawled atop the short pine, and shouted, "Come down here!" The second arrow flew before his shout had died out; there was a cry of pain, and Yanyan tumbled headlong to the ground.

"You fucking bastard," Hong Xi shrieked, "you've killed my wife. . . ."

People who had withdrawn from the grove came up with their lanterns and torches. "Is she dead?" they asked anxiously. "Are there feathers on her body?"

Without a word, Iron Mountain picked up a bucket of dog's blood and splashed its contents over Yanyan's body.

Iron Child

DURING THE GREAT LEAP FORWARD SMELTING CAMPAIGN, THE government mobilized 200,000 laborers to build a twelve-mile rail line; it was completed in two and a half months. The upper terminus linked with the Jiaoji trunk line at Gaomi Station; the lower terminus was located amid dozens of acres of Northeast Gaomi Township bushland.

Only four or five years old at the time, we were housed in a nursery school thrown up beside the public canteen. Consisting of a row of five rammed-earth buildings with thatched roofs, it was surrounded by saplings some six to seven feet tall, all strung together by heavy wire. Powerful dogs couldn't have bounded over it, let alone children like us. Our fathers, mothers, and older siblings — in fact, anyone who could handle a hoe or a shovel — were conscripted into the labor brigades. They ate and slept at the construction site, so we hadn't seen any of them for a very long time. Three skeletal old women were in charge of our "nursery school" confinement. Since all three had hawklike noses and sunken eyes, to us they looked like clones. Each day they prepared three cauldrons of porridge with wild greens: one in the morning, another at noon, and a third in the evening. We wolfed it down until our bellies were tight as little drums. Then after the meal, we went up to the fence to gaze at the scenery outside. New branches of willow and poplar sprang from the fence. Those with no green leaves were already rotting away; if they weren't removed, they sprouted yellow wood-ear fungi or little white mushrooms.

Feasting on the little mushrooms, we watched out-of-town laborers walk up and down the nearby road. They were grubby and listless, their hair a mess. As we searched for relatives among these laborers, tears in our eyes, we asked:

"Good uncle, have you seen my daddy?"

"Good uncle, have you seen my mommy?"

"Have you seen my brother?"

"Have you seen my sister?"

Some of them ignored us, as if they were deaf. Others cocked their heads and cast a fleeting glance, then shook their heads. But some ripped into us savagely:

"Come here, you little bastards!"

The three old women just sat in the doorways and paid no attention to us. The six-foot-high fence was too tall for us to climb over, and the spaces between the saplings were too narrow for us to wriggle through.

From our vantage point behind the fence we saw an earthen dragon rise up out of the distant field and watched hordes of people scramble busily up and down the earthen dragon, like ants swarming over a hill. The laborers who passed in front of our fence said that it was the roadbed for the rail line. Our kinfolk were a part of that human ant colony. From time to time people would suddenly stick thousands of red flags into the dragon; at other times they would suddenly insert thousands of white flags. But most of the time there were no flags. Some time later, a great many shiny objects appeared on top of the dragon. The passing laborers told us those were the steel rails.

One day, a sandy-haired young man came walking down the road. He was so tall we felt he could touch our fence by simply stretching out one of his long arms. When we asked about our relatives, he surprised us by walking up to the fence, squatting down, and cheerfully rubbing our noses, poking our bellies, and pinching our little peckers. He was the first person who had answered our calls. With a big smile he asked:

"What's your daddy's name?"

"Wang Fugui."

"Ah, Wang Fugui," he replied, rubbing his chin. "I know Wang Fugui."

"Do you know when he'll come get me?"

"He won't be coming. The other day, he was crushed while carrying steel rails."

"Waah . . ." One of the kids began to bawl.

"Have you seen my mommy?"

"What's your mommy's name?"

"Wan Xiuling."

"Ah, Wan Xiuling," he replied, rubbing his chin. "I know Wan Xiuling."

"Do you know when she'll come get me?"

"She won't be coming. The other day, she was crushed while carrying railroad ties."

"Waah . . ." Another of the kids began to bawl.

Before long, we were all bawling. The sandy-haired young man stood up and walked off whistling.

We cried from noon until sunset. We were still crying when

the old women called us to dinner. "What are you crying about?" they snarled. "If you don't stop, we'll throw you into Dead Man's Pit."

We had no idea where Dead Man's Pit was, but we knew it had to be a horrible place. We stopped crying.

The next day, we were back at the fence gazing at the scenery on the other side. At midmorning, several laborers rushed up to us carrying a door on which a bloody person was laid out. We couldn't tell if it was a man or a woman, but we could see *and* hear the blood dripping off the edge of the door and splattering on the ground.

One of the kids started crying, and in no time we were all crying, as if the person lying on the door were *our* relative.

After finishing our noon porridge, we went back to the fence, where we spotted the sandy-haired young man walking toward us in the custody of two swarthy, husky men armed with rifles. His hands were tied behind his back; his nose and eyes were bruised and swollen; his lips were bleeding. As he passed in front of us, he turned and gave us a wink, as if he couldn't have been happier.

We called out to him as one, but one of the guards jabbed him in the ribs with his rifle and shouted: "Get moving!"

On yet another morning, while we were leaning against the fence, we saw that the distant railway bed was suddenly alive with red flags, and we heard the clang of gongs and the beating of drums. All those people were shouting joyously for some reason. At lunchtime the old women gave each of us an egg and said: "Children, the rail line has been completed. The first train is due today. That means your daddies and mommies will be coming to get you. We've carried out our responsibility to look after you. These eggs are in celebration of the completion of the railway."

We were ecstatic. Our kinfolk weren't dead, after all. The sandy-haired young man had lied to us. No wonder they'd trussed him up and dragged him away.

Eggs were such a rare treat that the old women had to show us how to peel them first. Clumsily we peeled away the shells, only to find feathery little chicks inside. They chirped when we bit into them, and they bled. When we stopped eating, the old women took switches to us and demanded that we keep eating. We did.

When we were sprawled against the fence the next day, we saw even more red flags on the rail line. Later that afternoon, people on both sides of the tracks began to whoop and holler, as a giant object with thick smoke belching out of its head appeared. It was long and black and very big; it howled as it approached from the southwest. It was faster than a horse. It was the fastest thing we'd ever seen. We felt the earth move under our feet, and we were scared. Then we saw several women dressed all in white appear out of nowhere, clapping loudly and announcing:

"The train's coming! The train's here!"

The rumbling train headed off to the northeast, and we watched it until its tail end had disappeared from view.

After the train passed through, as promised, adults began showing up to pick up their children. Mutt was taken away, and so were Lamb, Pillar, and Beans, until I was the only one left.

The three old women led me out beyond the fence and said: "Go home!"

I'd long forgotten where I lived, and tearfully begged one of the old women to take me home. But she shoved me to one side, turned, and ran back indoors, closing the gate behind her. Then she secured it with a big, shiny brass lock. I stood outside the fence crying, screaming, and begging, but they ignored me. Through a crack in the fence, I watched the three identical old women set up a little pot in the yard, light some kindling under it, and pour in some light-green oil. As the kindling crackled and flames licked upward, the oil began to foam. When the foam dissipated, white smoke rose from the edges of the pot. The old women cracked some eggs open and flipped the feathery little chicks into the pot with makeshift chopsticks. They sizzled and rolled around in the hot oil, releasing the fragrance of cooked meat. The old women then picked the cooked chicks out of the oil, blew on them a time or two, and tossed them into their mouths. Their cheeks puffed out — first one side, then the other — and their lips smacked noisily. Tears flowed from their eyes, which were shut the whole time. They wouldn't open the gate, no matter how I cried or screamed. Soon my tears dried up and my voice failed me. I noticed a puddle of muddy water at the foot of an oily black tree. I went over to quench my thirst. But just as I was about to drink, I spotted a yellow toad beside the puddle. I also spotted a black snake with white dots running on its back. The toad and snake were locked in a fight. I was scared, but I was also very thirsty. So, holding my fear in check, I knelt down and scooped some water up with my hands. It dripped through my fingers. The snake had the toad's leg in its mouth, and a white liquid was oozing from the toad's head. The water was brackish, and slightly nauseating. I stood up, but didn't know where to go. I needed to cry, and so I did. But no tears came.

I saw trees, water, yellow toads, black snakes, fighting, fear, thirst, kneeling, cupping water, rank water, nausea, I cried, no tears. . . . Hey, what are you crying for, is your daddy dead? Is your mommy dead? Is everyone in your family dead? I turned my head. I saw the kid who asked me the questions. I saw that he was my height. I saw that he wasn't wearing any clothes. I saw that his skin was rusty. It seemed to me that he was an iron child. I saw that his eyes were black. And I saw that he was a boy, just like me.

He said, What are you crying for, Woody? I said, I'm not made of wood. He said, I'm going to call you Woody anyhow. He said, Woody come play with me over there on the railroad. He said there were lots of good things over there to look at, to eat, and to play with.

I told him a snake was about to swallow a toad. He said, Let it, don't bother it, snakes can suck out a kid's marrow.

He led me off in the direction of the railroad. It seemed so close, but we couldn't reach it. We walked and walked, looked and looked, but the railroad was as far away as ever, as if all the time we were walking, it was too. It took some doing, but we finally made it. By then my feet were killing me. I asked him his name. He said, My name is whatever you want it to be. I said, You look like a piece of rusty iron. He said, If you say I'm iron, then that's what I am. I said, Iron Child. He grunted a reply and laughed. I followed Iron Child up onto the railroad tracks. The roadbed was very steep. I saw that the rails were like two long serpents that had crawled from what must have been somewhere very far away. I imagined that if I stepped on one of them, it would start to wriggle, and that it would wrap its headless wooden tail around my legs. I stepped on one cautiously. The iron was cold, but it didn't wriggle and it didn't swish its tail.

I saw that the sun was about to set behind the mountain. It was very big and very red. A flock of white birds landed next to some water. I heard an eerie screech. Iron Child said that a train was coming. I saw that the iron wheels were red, and that iron arms were turning them. It felt to me as if the air rushing beneath the wheels could suck a person in. Iron Child waved to the train, as if it were his friend.

Hunger began to gnaw at me that night. Iron Child picked up a rusty iron bar and told me to eat it. I said I'm a human, how can I eat iron? Iron Child asked why a human can't eat iron. I'm a human and I can eat it. Just watch if you don't believe me. I watched as he put the iron bar up to his mouth and — *chomp chomp* — began to eat. Apparently, the iron bar was crisp and crunchy, and, by the looks of it, very tasty. I began to drool. I asked him where he'd learned to eat iron, and he said, Since when do you have to learn *how* to eat iron? I said I couldn't do it. And he asked me why not. Try it if you don't believe me. He held out the uneaten half of the steel bar and said, Try it. I said I was afraid I'd break my teeth. He said, Why? He said, There's nothing harder than people's teeth, and if you try it, you'll see what I mean. I took the iron bar hesitantly, put it up to my mouth, and licked it to see how it tasted. It was salty, sour, and rank, sort of like preserved fish. Take a bite, he said. I tried biting off a chunk and, to my surprise, succeeded with hardly any effort. As I began to chew, the flavor filled my mouth, tasting better and better until, before I knew it, I had greedily finished off the whole thing. Well? I wasn't lying, was I? No, you weren't, I said. You're a good kid, teaching me how to eat iron like that. I won't need to drink broth with greens anymore. He said, Anybody can eat iron, but people don't know that. I said, If they did, they wouldn't have to plant crops anymore, would they? He said, Do you think smelting iron is easier than planting crops? In fact, it's harder. Be sure you don't tell people how delicious iron is, because if they find out, they'll all start eating it, and there won't be any left for you and me. How come you let me in on this secret? I asked him. He said, I wanted to find a friend, since eating iron alone is no fun.

I followed him along the rails heading northeast. Now that I knew how to eat iron, I was no longer afraid of the rails. I muttered to myself, Iron rails, iron rails, don't get cocky, because if you do, I'll eat you up. Now that I'd finished off half an iron bar, I was no longer hungry, and my legs felt strong. Iron Child and I each walked down one of the rails. We walked so fast that in no time we reached a spot where the sky had turned red. Seven or eight huge ovens were spewing flames into the air, and I could smell the fresh, tantalizing aroma of iron. He said, Up ahead there is where they smelt iron and steel. Who knows, maybe that's where your daddy and mommy are. I said, I don't care if they're there or not.

We walked and walked until the railway came to an abrupt end. We were surrounded by head-high weeds that were home to heaps of rusty scrap iron and steel. Several crushed trains lay on their sides in the weeds, their scrap iron and steel cargo spilled on the ground beside them. Walking on a bit farther, we ran across crowds of people squatting down and eating amid the iron and steel. Flames from the smelting ovens turned their faces bright red. It was mealtime. What were they eating? Meaty dumplings and sweet potatoes with eggs. The food must have been delicious, the way their cheeks were all puffed out, as if they had the mumps. But to me the stench of those meaty dumplings and sweet potatoes and eggs was worse than dog shit, and it made me so sick to my stomach I had to run downwind to avoid it. Just then a man and a woman in the crowd stood up and shouted:

"Gousheng!"

They scared me at first. But then I recognized them as my daddy and mommy. They came stumbling toward me, and it suddenly dawned on me what horrifying people they were, at least as horrifying as the three old women at the "nursery school." I could smell the stench on their bodies, worse than dog shit. So when they reached out to grab me, I turned and ran away. They lit out after me. I didn't dare turn my head to look back, but I could feel their fingers each time they touched my scalp. And that's when I heard my good friend, Iron Child, yell at me from somewhere in front:

"Woody, Woody, head for the scrap iron heap!"

I watched as his dark red body flashed for an instant in the scrap iron heap, and then vanished from sight. I ran into the heap, stepping on woks, hoes, plows, rifles, cannons, and other things as I climbed to the top. Iron Child waved to me from inside a drainpipe. With a quick hunch of my shoulders, I scrambled inside. It was black as night, and I was surrounded by the fragrance of rust. I couldn't see a thing, but I felt an icy hand grab hold of my hand, and I knew it was Iron Child. He whispered:

"Don't be afraid. Follow me. They can't see us in here."

So I crawled along behind him. I had no idea where the pipe, with all its twists and turns, led to, so I kept crawling until I saw a light up ahead. I followed Iron Child out of the pipe and onto the treads of an abandoned tank; from there we crawled up to the turret. White five-pointed stars had been painted on the turret, from which the rusted, pitted barrel of a cannon protruded, pointing up at an angle. Iron Child said he wanted to crawl into the turret, but the hatch was rusted shut. Iron Child said:

"Let's bite off the screws."

Still on our hands and knees, we circled the hatch, biting off all the rusty screws, quickly chewing them up, until we'd broken through. We tossed the hatch away. The turret was made of soft metal, sort of like overripe peaches. Once we were inside, we settled into the soft, spongy iron seats. Iron Child showed me a tiny opening, through which I could see my parents. They were crawling over a distant heap of scrap iron, tossing objects around and making loud clanging noises that blended with their tearful shouts:

"Gousheng, Gousheng, my son, come out, come out and have some meaty dumplings and sweet potatoes and eggs. . . ."

They looked like strangers to me, and when I heard them trying to tempt me with meaty dumplings and sweet potatoes and eggs, I sneered contemptuously.

Finally they gave up looking for me and headed back.

After crawling out of the turret, we straddled the barrel of the cannon, a great vantage point to watch the flames leaping out of ovens, some near and some far, and all the people scurrying around them. Picking up iron woks, with a One — Two — Three, they tossed them into the air and then watched as they broke apart when they hit the ground. They then smashed them to pieces with sledgehammers. The sweet aroma of burned iron filings drifted over to us; my stomach started to rumble. Apparently sensing what was on my mind, Iron Child said:

"Come on, Woody, let's get one of those woks. Iron woks are delicious."

We sneaked into the glow, where we selected a great big wok, picked it up, and ran off with it, so shocking the men who saw us that they dropped their hammers. Some of them even took off running.

"Iron demons!" they shouted as they ran. "The iron demons have come!"

By that time we'd made it to the top of a heap of scrap iron and had begun breaking the wok into edible pieces. It was much tastier than the iron bar.

As we were feasting on our iron wok, we saw a man with a gimpy leg and a holstered revolver on his hip limp over and smack the men who were shouting "iron demons."

"Bastards," he cursed them. "Your damned rumors are creating a disturbance! A fox can turn into a demon, and so can a tree. But whoever heard of iron turning into demons?"

The men replied as if with one voice:

"We're not lying, Political Instructor. We were smashing some iron woks when a pair of iron kids, covered with rust, came rushing out of the shadows, snatched one of the woks, and ran off with it. They simply vanished."

"Where did they run off to?" the gimpy man asked.

"The scrap iron heap," the men answered.

"You fucking rumor-mongers!" the gimpy man said. "How could there be kids in this desolate spot?"

"That's why we were scared."

The gimpy man drew his pistol and fired three shots into the scrap iron heap — *clang clang clang.* Golden sparks flew from the scrap iron.

Iron Child said:

"Woody, let's take his gun away from him and eat it, what do you say?"

I said:

"What if we can't get it away from him?"

Iron Child said:

"Wait here. I'll go get it."

Iron Child climbed lightly down off the scrap heap and crawled on his belly through the weeds. The people out in the light couldn't see him, but I could. When I saw him crawl up behind the gimpy man, I picked up a piece of iron plate and banged it against the wok.

"Hear that?" the men shouted. "The iron demons are over there!"

Just as the gimpy man raised his pistol to fire, Iron Child jumped up and snatched it out of his hand.

The men shouted:

"An iron demon!"

The gimpy man fell down on his backside.

"Help!" he screamed. "Catch that spy —"

Pistol in hand, Iron Child crawled up next to me.

"Well?" he said.

I told him how great he was, which made him very happy. He bit off the barrel and handed it to me.

"Eat," he said.

I took a bite. It tasted like gunpowder. I spit it out and complained:

"It tastes terrible. It's no good."

He bit off a chunk above the handle to taste it.

"You're right," he said, "it's no good. I'm going to toss it back to him."

He flung the pistol down at the feet of the gimpy man.

I flung the partially eaten barrel at the same spot.

The gimpy man picked up the two pieces of his pistol, gaped at them, and started to howl. He tossed the things away and hobbled off as fast he could go. From where we sat on the scrap heap we laughed our heads off over the funny way he ran.

Late that night a narrow beam of light pierced the darkness off to the southwest, accompanied by a loud chugging noise. Another train was coming.

We watched as it steamed up to the end of the tracks, where it plowed into another train already there. The cars of the train accordioned into one another, noisily dumping the iron they were hauling to the side of the tracks.

There would be no more trains after that. I asked if there were any parts of the train that were tasty. He said the wheels were the best. So we started eating one of them, but stopped when we were halfway through it.

We also went down to the smelting ovens to find some newly smelted iron, but none of it tasted as good as the rusty iron we were used to.

We slept on the scrap iron heap during the day, then made

life difficult for the smelters at night, sending them scurrying off in fear.

One night, we went out to frighten the men who were smashing woks. Spotting a rusty red wok in the flames of one of the ovens, we ran over. But we no sooner got our hands on it than we heard a loud *whoosh* as a rope net dropped over us.

We attacked the net with our teeth, but no matter how hard we tried, we couldn't bite through the rope.

"We caught them," they cried out ecstatically, "we caught them!"

Soon afterward, they scraped our rusty bodies with sandpaper. It hurt, it hurt like hell!

The Cure

THAT AFTERNOON, THE ARMED WORK DETACHMENT POSTED A notice on the whitewashed wall of Ma Kuisan's home, which faced the street; it announced the following morning's executions at the usual place: the southern bridgehead of the Jiao River. All able-bodied villagers were to turn out for educational purposes. There were so many executions that year that people had lost interest in them, and the only way to draw a crowd was to make attendance mandatory.

The room was still pitch-black when Father got up to light the bean-oil lamp. After putting on his lined jacket, he woke me up and tried to get me out of bed, but it was so cold all I wanted to do was stay under the warm covers — which Father finally pulled back. "Get up," he said. "The armed work detachment likes to get their business over with early. If we're late, we'll miss our chance."

I followed Father out the gate. The eastern sky was growing light. The streets were icy cold and deserted; winds from the northwest had swept the dust clean during the night; and the gray roadway was clearly visible. My fingers and toes were so cold it felt as if they were being chewed by a cat. As we passed the Ma family compound, where the armed work detachment was quartered, we noticed a light in the window and heard the sound of a bellows. Father said softly, "Step it up. The work detachment is getting breakfast."

Father dragged me up to the top of the riverbank; from there, we could see the dark outline of the stone bridge and patches of ice in the hollows of the riverbed. I asked, "Where are we going to hide, Father?"

"Under the bridge."

It was deserted under the bridge and pitch-black, not to mention freezing cold. My scalp tingled, so I asked Father, "How come my scalp is tingling?"

"Mine, too," he said. "They've shot so many people here that the ghosts of the wronged are everywhere."

I detected the movement of furry creatures in the darkness under the bridge. "There they are!" I shouted.

"Those aren't wronged ghosts," Father said. "They're dogs that feed on the dead."

I shrank back until I bumped into the bone-chilling cold of a bridge piling. All I could think about was Grandma, whose eyes were so clouded over with cataracts she was all but blind. The sky would be completely light once the cold glare from the three western stars slanted into the space under the bridge. Father lit his pipe; the fragrant smell of tobacco quickly enveloped us. My lips were turning numb. "Father, can I go out and run around? I'm freezing."

Father's reply was, "Grate your teeth. The armed work detachment shoots their prisoners when the morning sun is still red."

"Who are they shooting this morning, Father?"

"I don't know," Father said. "But we'll find out soon enough. I hope they shoot some young ones."

"Why?"

"Young people have young bodies. Better results."

There was more I wanted to ask, but Father was already losing his patience. "No more questions. Everything we say down here can be heard up there."

While we were talking, the sky turned fish-belly white. The village dogs had formed a pack and were barking loudly, but they couldn't drown out the wailing sounds of women. Father emerged from our hiding spot and stood for a moment in the riverbed, cocking his ear in the direction of the village. Now I was really getting nervous. The scavenger dogs prowling the space under the bridge were glaring at me as if they wanted to tear me limb from limb. I don't know what kept me from getting out of there as fast as I could. Father returned at a crouch. I saw his lips quiver in the dim light of dawn but couldn't tell if he was cold or scared. "Did you hear anything?" I asked.

"Keep quiet," Father whispered. "They'll be here soon. I could hear them tying up the condemned."

I moved up close to Father and sat down on a clump of weeds. By listening carefully, I could hear a gong in the village, mixed in with a man's raspy voice: "Villagers — go to the southern bridgehead to watch the execution — shoot the tyrannical landlord Ma Kuisan — his wife — puppet village head Luan Fengshan — orders of armed work detachment Chief Zhang — those who don't go will be punished as collaborators."

I heard Father grumble softly, "Why are they doing this to Ma Kuisan? Why shoot him? He's the last person they should shoot."

I wanted to ask Father why they shouldn't shoot Ma Kuisan,

but before I could open my mouth, I heard the crack of a rifle, and a bullet went whizzing far off, way up into the sky somewhere. Then came the sound of horse hoofs heading our way, all the way up to the bridgehead; when they hit the flooring, they clattered like a passing whirlwind. Father and I shrank back and looked at the slivers of sunlight filtering down through cracks between the stones; we were both frightened and not quite sure just what was happening. After about half the time it takes to smoke a pipeful, we heard people coming toward us, shouting and clamoring. They stopped. I heard a man whose voice sounded like a duck's quack: "Let him go, damn it. We'll never catch him."

Whoever it was fired a couple of shots in the direction of the hoofbeats. The sound echoed off the walls where we were hiding; my ears rang, and there was a strong smell of gunpowder.

Again the quack: "What the fuck are you shooting at? By now, he's in the next county."

"I never thought he'd do anything like that," someone else said. "Chief Zhang, he must be a farmhand."

"He's a paid running dog of the landlord class, if you ask me," the duck quacked.

Someone walked to the railing and started pissing over the side of the bridge. The smell was rank and overpowering.

"Come on, let's head back," the duck quacked. "We've got an execution to attend to."

Father whispered to me that the man who sounded like a duck was the chief of the armed work detachment, given the added responsibility by the district government of rooting out traitors to the Party; he was referred to as Chief Zhang.

The sky was starting to turn pink on the eastern horizon, where thin, low-hanging clouds slowly came into view; before long, they, too, were pink. Now it was light enough to make out some frozen dog turds on the ground of our hiding place, that and some shredded clothing, clumps of hair, and a chewed-up human skull. It was so repulsive I had to look away. The riverbed was as dry as a bone except for an ice-covered puddle here and there; clumps of dew-specked weeds stood on the sloped edges. The northern winds had died out; trees on the embankments stood stiff and still in the freezing air. I turned to look at Father; I could see his breath. Time seemed to stand still. Then Father said, "Here they come."

The arrival of the execution party at the bridgehead was announced by the frantic beating of a gong and muted footsteps. Then a booming voice rang out: "Chief Zhang, Chief Zhang, I've been a good man all my life . . ."

Father whispered, "That's Ma Kuisan."

Another voice, this one flat and cracking with emotion: "Chief Zhang, be merciful. . . . We drew lots to see who would be village head; I didn't want the job. . . . We drew lots; I got the short straw — my bad luck. . . . Chief Zhang, be merciful, and spare my dog life. . . . I've got an eighty-year-old mother at home I have to take care of. . . ."

Father whispered, "That's Luan Fengshan."

After that, a high-pitched voice said, "Chief Zhang, when you moved into our home, I fed you well and gave you the best wine we had. I even let our eighteen-year-old daughter look after your needs. Chief Zhang, you don't have a heart of steel, do you?"

Father said, "That's Ma Kuisan's wife."

Finally, I heard a woman bellow "Wu — la — ah — ya —"

Father whispered, "That's Luan Fengshan's wife, the mute."

In a calm, casual tone, Chief Zhang said, "We're going to shoot you whether you make a fuss or not, so you might as well stop all that shouting. Everybody has to die sometime. You might as well get it over with early so you can come back as somebody else."

That's when Ma Kuisan announced loudly to the crowd, "All you folks, young and old, I, Ma Kuisan, have never done you any harm. Now I'm asking you to speak up for me. . . ."

Several people fell noisily to their knees and began to plead in desperation, "Be merciful, Chief Zhang. Let them live. They're honest folk, all of them. . . ."

A youthful male voice shouted above the noise, "Chief Zhang, I say we make these four dog bastards get down on their hands right here on the bridge and kowtow to us a hundred times. Then we give them back their dog lives. What do you say?"

"That's some idea you've got there, Gao Renshan!" Chief Zhang replied menacingly. "Are you suggesting that I, Zhang Qude, am some sort of avenging monster? It sounds to me like you've been head of the militia long enough! Now get up, fellow villagers. It's too cold to be kneeling like that. The policy is clear. Nobody can save them now, so everybody get up."

"Fellow villagers, speak up for me —" Ma Kuisan pleaded.

"No more dawdling," Chief Zhang cut him short. "It's time."

"Clear out, make some room!" Several young men at the

bridgehead, almost certainly members of the armed work detachment, were clearing the bridge of the kneeling citizens.

Then Ma Kuisan sent his pleas heavenward: "Old man in the sky, are you blind? Am I, Ma Kuisan, being repaid for a lifetime of good with a bullet in the head? Zhang Qude, you son of a bitch, you will not die in bed, count on it. You son of a bitch —"

"Get on with it!" Chief Zhang bellowed. "Or do you like to hear him spout his poison?"

Running footsteps crossed the bridge above us. Through cracks between the stones, I caught glimpses of the people.

"Kneel!" someone on the southern edge of the bridge demanded. "Clear the way, everybody," came a shout from the northern edge.

Pow — pow — pow — three shots rang out.

The explosions bored into my eardrums and made them throb until I thought I'd gone deaf. By then, the sun had climbed above the eastern horizon, rimmed by a blood-red halo that spread to clouds looking like canopies of gigantic fir trees. A large, bulky human form came tumbling slowly down from the bridge above, cloudlike in its shifting movements; when it hit the icy ground below, it regained its natural heft and thudded to a stop. Crystalline threads of blood oozed from the head.

Panic and confusion at the northern bridgehead — it sounded to me like the frantic dispersal of villagers who had been forcibly mobilized as witnesses to the executions. It didn't sound as if the armed work detachment took out after the deserters?

Once again, footsteps rushed across the bridge from north

to south, followed by the shout of "Kneel!" at the southern bridgehead and "Clear the way!" at the northern. Then three more shots — the body of Luan Fengshan, hatless and wearing a ragged padded coat, tumbled head over heels down the riverbank, first bumping into Ma Kuisan, then rolling off to the side.

After that, things were simplified considerably. A volley of shots preceded the sound and sight of two disheveled female corpses tumbling down, arms and legs flying, and crashing into the bodies of their menfolk.

I held tightly to Father's arm, feeling something warm and wet against my padded trousers.

At least a half-dozen people were standing on the bridge directly overhead, and it seemed to me that their weight was pushing the rock flooring down on top of us. Their thunderous shouts were nearly deafening: "Shall we check out the bodies, Chief?"

"What the hell for? Their brains are splattered all over the place. If the Jade Emperor himself came down now, he couldn't save them."

"Let's go! Old Guo's wife has fermented bean curd and oil fritters waiting for us."

They crossed the bridge, heading north, their footsteps sounding like an avalanche. The rock flooring, creaking and shifting, could have come crashing down at any moment. Or so it seemed to me.

The quiet returned.

Father nudged me. "Don't stand there like an idiot. Let's do it."

I looked around me, but nothing made sense. Even my own father seemed familiar, but I couldn't place him.

"Huh?" I'm sure that's all I managed to say: "Huh?"

"Have you forgotten?" Father said. "We're here to get a cure for your grandmother. We have to move fast, before the body snatchers show up."

The words were still echoing in my ears when I spotted seven or eight wild dogs, in a variety of colors, dragging their long shadows up off the riverbed in our direction; they were baying at us. All I could think of was how they had turned and fled at the first gunshot, accompanied by their own terrified barks.

I watched Father kick loose several bricks and fling them at the approaching dogs. They scurried out of the way. Then he took out a carving knife from under his coat and waved it in the air to threaten the dogs. Beautiful silvery arcs of light flashed around Father's dark silhouette. The dogs kept their distance for the time being. Father tightened the cord around his waist and rolled up his sleeves. "Keep an eye out for me," he said.

Like an eagle pouncing on its prey, Father dragged the women's bodies away, then rolled Ma Kuisan over so he was facing up. Then he fell to his knees and kowtowed to the body. "Second Master Ma," he intoned softly, "loyalty and filiality have their limits. I hate to do this to you."

I watched Ma Kuisan reach up and wipe his bloody face. "Zhang Qude," he said with a trace of a smile, "you will not die in bed."

Father tried to unbutton Ma Kuisan's leather coat with one

hand but was shaking too much to manage. "Hey, Second Son," I heard him say, "hold the knife for me."

I recall reaching out to take the knife from him, but he was already holding it in his mouth as he struggled with the yellow buttons down Ma Kuisan's chest. Round, golden yellow, and as big as mung beans, they were nearly impossible to separate from the cloth loops encircling them. Growing increasingly impatient, Father ripped them loose and jerked the coat open, revealing a white kidskin lining. A satin vestlike garment had the same kind of buttons, so Father ripped them loose, too. After the vest came a red silk stomacher. I heard Father snort angrily. I have to admit that I was surprised when I saw the strangely alluring clothing the fat old man — he was over fifty — wore under his regular clothes. But Father seemed absolutely irate; he ripped the thing off the body and flung it to one side. Now at last, Ma Kuisan's rounded belly and flat chest were out in the open. Father reached out his hand but then jumped to his feet, his face the color of gold. "Second Son," he said, "tell me if he's got a heartbeat."

I recall bending over and laying my hand on his chest. It was no stronger than a rabbit's, but that heart was still beating.

"Second Master Ma," my father said, "your brains have spilled out on the ground, and even the Jade Emperor couldn't save you now, so help me be a filial son, won't you?"

Father took the knife from between his teeth and moved it up and down the chest area, trying to find the right place to cut. I saw him press down, but the skin sprang back undamaged, like a rubber tire. He pressed down again with the same result. Father fell to his knees. "Second Master Ma, I know you didn't deserve to die, but if you've got a bone to pick, it's with Chief Zhang, not me. I'm just trying to be a filial son."

Father had pressed down with the knife only twice, but already his forehead was all sweaty, the stubble on his chin white with icy moisture. The damned wild dogs were inching closer and closer to us — their eyes were red as hot coals, the fur on their necks was standing straight up, like porcupine quills, and their razor-sharp fangs were bared. I turned to Father. "Hurry, the dogs are coming."

He stood up, waved the knife above his head, and charged the wild dogs like a madman, driving them back about half the distance an arrow flies. Then he ran back, breathless, and said loudly, "Second Master, if I don't cut you open, the dogs will do it with their teeth. I think you'd rather it be me than them."

Father's jaw set, his eyes bulged. With a sense of determination, he brought his hand down; the knife cut into Ma Kuisan's chest with a slurping sound, all the way to the hilt. He jerked the knife to the side, releasing a stream of blackish blood, but the rib cage stopped his motion. "I lost my head," he said as he pulled the knife out, wiped the blade on Ma Kuisan's leather coat, gripped the handle tightly, and opened Ma Kuisan's chest.

I heard a gurgling noise and watched the knife slice through the fatty tissue beneath the skin and release the squirming, yellowish intestines into the opening, like a snake, like a mass of eels; there was a hot, fetid smell.

Fishing out the intestines by the handful, Father looked like a very agitated man: he pulled and he tugged; he cursed and he swore; and finally, he ran out of intestines, leaving Ma Kuisan with a hollow abdomen.

"What are you looking for, Father?" I recall asking him anxiously.

"The gall bladder. Where the hell is his gall bladder?"

Father cut through the diaphragm and fished around until he had his hand around the heart — still nice and red. Then he dug out the lungs. Finally, alongside the liver, he discovered the egg-sized gall bladder. Very carefully, he separated it from the liver with the tip of his knife, then held it in the palm of his hand to examine it. The thing was moist and slippery and, in the sunlight, had a sheen. Sort of like a piece of fine purple jade.

Father handed me the gall bladder. "Hold this carefully while I take out Luan Fengshan's gall bladder."

This time, Father performed like an experienced surgeon: deft, quick, exact. First he cut away the hemp cord that was all Luan Fengshan could afford for a belt. Then he opened the front of his ragged coat and held the scrawny, bony chest still with his foot as he made four or five swift cuts. After that, he cleared away all the obstructions, stuck in his hand, and, as if it were the pit of an apricot, removed Luan's gall bladder.

"Let's get out of here," Father said.

We ran up the riverbank, where the dogs were fighting over the coils of intestines. Only a trace of red remained on the edges of the sun; its blinding rays fell on all exposed objects, large and small.

Grandma had advanced cataracts, according to Luo Dashan, the miracle worker. The source of her illness was heat rising from her three visceral cavities. The cure would have to be something very cold and very bitter. The physician lifted up the hem of his floor-length coat and was heading out the door when Father begged him to prescribe something.

"Hmm, prescribe something. . . ." Miracle worker Luo told Father to get a pig's gall bladder and have his mother take the squeezings, which should clear her eyes a little.

"How about a goat's gall bladder?" Father asked.

"Goats are fine," the physician said, "so are bears. Now if you could get your hands on a human gall bladder . . . ha, ha. . . . Well, I wouldn't be surprised if your mother's eyesight returned to normal."

Father squeezed the liquid from Ma Kuisan's and Luan Fengshan's gall bladders into a green tea bowl, which he offered up to Grandma in both hands. She raised it to her lips and touched the liquid with the tip of her tongue. "Gouzi's daddy," she said, "this gall is awfully bitter. Where'd it come from?"

Father replied, "It's gall from a *ma* [horse] and a *luan*."

"A *ma* and a *luan*, you say? I know what a *ma* is, but what's a *luan*?"

Unable to stop myself, I blurted out, "Grandma, it's human gall, it's from Ma Kuisan and Luan Fengshan. Daddy scooped out their bladders!"

With a shriek, Grandma fell backward onto the brick bed, dead as a stone.

Love Story

THAT AUTUMN THE TEAM LEADER SENT FIFTEEN-YEAR-OLD JUNIOR and sixty-five-year-old Guo Three out into the fields to man the waterwheel. Why? To wheel water. For what? To irrigate the cabbage crop. A "sent-down" city girl named He Liping, in her mid-twenties, was in charge of the irrigation ditches.

Once the thirteenth solar period — Autumn Beginning — arrives, the cabbage must be watered daily, or the roots will rot. In his orders, the team leader spared the three workers from mustering for duty each morning, since they had to go into the fields to water the cabbage right after breakfast. Which they did, from Autumn Beginning to Frost's Descent, the eighteenth solar period. Naturally, irrigation wasn't all they did; other tasks included spreading fertilizer, controlling pests, binding up drooping cabbage leaves with sweet potato sprouts, and so on. They took four breaks a day, each lasting half an hour or so. The city girl, He Liping, owned a watch. Frost's Descent arrived, and the temperature plunged; the cabbage curled up into balls, bringing an end to the team's irrigation duties.

They dismantled the waterwheel and transported it back to the production team compound on a handcart, where they turned it over to the storekeeper. After a cursory inspection, he sent them on their way.

The next morning, right after breakfast, they stood beneath the iron bell to wait for new orders from the team leader. He had the old-timer, Guo Three, hitch up the ox to till the bean field and sent Junior out to re-sow millet at the farthest edge of the production team land. "What about me, Team Leader?" He Liping asked. "Go with Junior. You can prepare the furrows while he spreads the seeds."

One of the commune wags extended the team leader's orders: "Junior," he teased, "take good aim on He Liping's furrow. Make sure you spread your seed where it belongs."

While the crowd laughed raucously, Junior felt his heart pound against his chest wall. He sneaked a look at He Liping, who stood stony-faced, obviously unhappy. That really upset him. "Fuck your old lady, Old Qi!" he cursed his playful tormentor.

The cabbage patch was located on the east side of the village, next to the pond. Swollen with rainwater, the pond was a breeding ground for algae and moss, making it greener than green and deeper than anyone could imagine. The main reason the production team had chosen that site to plant cabbage was the proximity of all that water. There was nothing wrong with well water, of course, but it wasn't nearly as good as the water in the pond. Mounted high on the pond's edge, the waterwheel looked like a poolside arbor. Junior and the oldster Guo Three stood on a shaky wooden footrest and turned the iron winch handles, one up and one down, squeaking and twisting as water flowed steadily. It didn't rain from Autumn's Beginning to Frost's Descent, not once. The skies were washed clean by the glare of the sun, day in and day out, and the surface of the pond stayed placid, wind or no wind. Clouds in the sky were matched by clouds in the pond that were, if anything, clearer than those above. Sometimes Junior stared at the clouds until he was in a world of his own, and forgot to turn the winch, to Guo Three's vocal displeasure: "Wake up, Junior!" At the northern tip of the pond stood a solitary patch of marshy reeds no larger than a sleeping mat, looking like a mirage. The reeds grew yellower each day, until in the bright rays of the morning sun and slanting rays of the setting sun, they seemed brushed by gold.

Let's say a really large, bright red dragonfly lands on one of the golden leaves, forming a dreamy plateau with the pond and the reeds. Then a dozen or so ducks and seven or eight geese, all pure white, glide across the surface. From time to time the long-necked ganders mount female geese, at other times they grant similar favors to female ducks. Junior stands transfixed when the ganders do that, and of course he forgets to turn the winch, which invariably earns abuse from Guo Three: "Just what are you thinking about?" Quickly averting his eyes from the naughty ganders and ducks, he starts turning the winch extra hard. Out the water gushes, as the rickety waterwheel creaks and groans. Amid the clanks of the chain, Junior hears Guo Three gripe, "Little peach-fuzz doesn't have a man's pecker yet, but his head hasn't gotten the message!" Junior is deeply shamed. The lovely bright red dragonfly soaring above the pond has got a new name, thanks to old-timer Guo Three: Little Bride.

He Liping was a tall girl, taller than Guo Three, and she knew martial arts. In fact, they learned, she had performed in

Europe with a team of martial arts experts. Most people agreed that she could have made quite a name for herself if not for the Cultural Revolution. Too bad. Ruined by her family background. Proof of the two most frequently heard versions — that her father was a capitalist and that he was a capitalist-roader — was not actively sought, since the difference between the two is negligible. It was enough to know that her background was bad.

He Liping was a taciturn girl who, in the eyes of the villagers, knew her place. She had been sent to the countryside with lots of other educated city kids: some ended up by going on to school, others took jobs, the rest returned to their hometowns. Only she was left behind, and everyone knew it was because of her background.

Only once did He Liping demonstrate her martial arts skills, and that was soon after showing up in the village. Junior was no more than eight or nine at the time. Back then, "Mao Zedong Thought" propaganda meetings were common occurrences. The city kids were terrific talkers and singers, and some played the harmonica or flute or two-string *huqin*. There was a lot going on in the village back then: during the day the commune members worked in the fields, and at night they made revolution. With all the excitement, every day seemed like New Year's Eve to Junior. One night, very much like all the other nights, everyone poured out of the dining hall after dinner to make revolution. On the dirt platform, which had a post stuck in both ends to support gas lamps, the city kids filled the platform with their songs and instruments. Junior recalled that suddenly the young emcee shouted above the din: "Poor and lower-middle peasant comrades, our great leader

Chairman Mao instructs us: Power comes out of the barrel of a gun! Now please turn your attention to He Liping, who will demonstrate her 'nine-stage plum-blossom' spear routine."

Junior recalled that everyone applauded like crazy, anticipating the arrival of He Leping. They didn't have to wait long. She came out in a skintight red outfit and white plastic sandals, with her hair coiled atop her head. All the hot-blooded young men buzzed about her pert breasts, which nearly popped out of their tight wrappings. Some said they were real, others said they weren't. One of the latter insisted that she was wearing plastic cups. She stood on the stage, striking a martial pose, red-tasseled spear in hand. With her chin held high, her back arched, and her dark eyes sparkling, she cut quite a figure. Then she began to twirl her spear, until all anyone could see on the stage was a red blur, and no one could follow the twists and turns of her lithe body. Finally she stopped spinning and stood ramrod straight with her spear, looking like a column of red smoke. The audience seemed frozen in place for a moment, no one making a peep. Then, suddenly snapping out of their trance, they clapped politely, as if physically drained.

It was a sleepless night for the young men of the village.

The next day, as members of the commune sprawled on the ground to rest, He Liping and her "nine-stage plum-blossom" were all anyone talked about. Someone said the girl's performance was like a flower stand: attractive but hardly practical; but someone else said it was like the wind, so fast she could keep four or five people at bay at the same time, and how much more practical can you get? Then someone said that anybody who took a girl like her for a wife was in for real trouble, that he'd get off lucky if all she did was beat him, that she definitely was a woman who rode her husband in bed, that no man, even one as strong as an ox, was a match for her "nine-stage plum-blossom." At that point the tone of the discussion took a dive, and Junior, who was working with the older men at the time, was a little embarrassed and a little upset by what was being said.

He Liping performed her "nine-stage plum-blossom" only that one time. Apparently, a report was sent to the commune revolutionary committee, from which emerged a pronouncement that spears belonged only in the hands of descendants of the reddest of the red. How could anybody have allowed one to fall into the hands of someone who came from the five black categories?

Head bowed and utterly demoralized, He Liping worked silently alongside the other members of the commune. Then when all the other city kids spread their wings and flew off to their homes, she felt all alone and lonely, and that gained her plenty of sympathy. The team leader started giving her light duties. No one gave a thought to whether or not she should get married. The young male villagers hadn't forgotten her skills with a spear, and stayed clear of her.

One day she sat on the footrest of the waterwheel dangling her legs and staring at the placid green water on the pond. Junior, who was resting at the edge of the pond, couldn't keep his eyes off her darkly tanned face; high, bony nose; and eyes so dark and large there didn't seem to be any room for the whites. Her eyebrows swept sharply toward her temple hair, and there was a large, dark red mole squarely in the center of her left brow. Her teeth were very white, her mouth quite large, and her hair so thick and bushy that Junior couldn't see any of her scalp. She was dressed that day in a blue gabardine army-style tunic that was nearly white from all the washings; a snowy white wedge of skin and the lacy trim of an undershirt poked out above the unbuttoned collar of her tunic. As his gaze continued downward, Junior grew so flustered he had to turn his face toward the cabbage patch, over which a pair of butterflies frolicked. But he didn't see the butterflies, since his head was filled with images of He Liping's tunic pockets, which were thrust outward by the arching breasts behind them.

The oldster Guo Three was not a true farmer. Junior had heard people say he once worked as a "big teapot" in a Qingdao whorehouse when he was young. Junior didn't know what a "big teapot" did, and he was too shy to ask.

Guo Three, now wifeless, lived a bachelor's existence, although there was talk that he had something going with the wife of Li Gaofa, who wore her glossy hair pulled straight back above a large fair-skinned face. Broad in the beam, she waddled like a duck when she walked. She lived close enough to the pond so that Junior and Guo Three could see her yard when they worked the waterwheel. A large, black, and very mean dog prowled the area.

They had been irrigating the cabbage patch for four days when the Li woman came over to the pond carrying a straw basket. She sidled up to the edge of the pond, a little at a time, until she was right beside the waterwheel. "Ge-ge-ge-ge," she tittered.

"Third Uncle," she said to Guo Three, "the team leader gave you the best job."

Guo Three giggled. "It may look easy, but it's not. Just ask Junior."

After working the wheel for several days in a row, Junior

had noticed that his arms were, in fact, starting to ache. He just grinned and looked down on the Li woman's greasy, swept-back hair, and had a funny feeling. He didn't like her, not at all.

"That gimpy devil I'm married to was sent on a rock-gathering expedition to South Mountain," the Li woman said. "He took his bedroll, since he won't be back for a month. I think the team leader's out to get me. With all the able-bodied young bachelors around here, why'd he send the gimpy devil?"

Junior noticed that Guo Three was blinking nervously and heard a dry chuckle rattle around in his throat. "He was show-ing how much he valued you folks," he said.

"Hah!" the Li woman snorted angrily. "The old jackass is just out to get me."

This time the oldster Guo Three held his tongue. The Li woman stretched lazily and squinted up at the sun. "Third Uncle, it's nearly noon. Time for a break."

Guo Three shielded his eyes with his hand and looked up at the sun. "Yes, I guess it is." He let go of the winch handle and shouted into the field, "Little He, break time!"

"Third Uncle," the Li woman said, "that dog of ours has been off his feed the last few days. How about taking a look at him for me?"

Guo Three glanced at Junior. "After I've smoked a pipeful," he said.

As she walked off, the Li woman looked over her shoulder and said, "Don't be too long."

"I know, I know," he replied with affected agitation, as he took out his tobacco pouch and his pipe. "How about you, lad?" he said to Junior with uncharacteristic warmth. "Smoke?" Then he stuck the pipe into his mouth without waiting for an answer. Junior watched him light it. "I'm getting old," he said as he thumped his waist with his fists. "It doesn't take much for these old bones to start aching."

Guo Three walked off in the footsteps of the Li woman. But instead of watching either of them, Junior turned back toward the cabbage patch, where He Liping was standing stock still on a field embankment, hoe in hand. The sight saddened Junior. The water in the pond, polluted by the leather scoops of the waterwheel, turned muddy and rank-smelling. He could almost taste it. The metal pipe gave out a hollow cough, the chain clanked once or twice, the handlebar turned backward a time or two, and the water drained back into the pond. The waterwheel fell silent.

As he sat on the wooden plank and let his legs dangle over the edge, Junior noticed that his hands had rubbed the rust off the handlebar. On that sunny day, water flowing sluggishly down the furrows in the cabbage patch caught the sun's rays and shone like splintered silver. The plants seemed frozen in place, and so did the high riverbank at the far end of the cabbage patch and the persimmon tree atop it, whose leaves were already starting to turn a fiery red. Junior looked westward just in time to see Guo Three stride into the yard of the Li home, where the big black dog barked once, then wagged his tail in welcome. Guo Three and the dog went inside together. Purple flowers were blooming on lentils climbing a trellis in the yard. Ripples rose on the surface of the pond, where a duck quacked and a goose honked. Two pairs of wings flapped against the water. The white long-necked gander pushed the duck under the water, and when they surfaced, he was riding on her back. Junior jumped to the ground, scooped up a handful of mud, and flung it at the gander. But it was, after all, just mud, which fell apart before it even hit the water, raising only some tiny splashes. The duck, still mounted by the gander, sped around the pond.

Junior was visited by emotions he'd never known before. He felt chilled, and the mist above the pond raised goose bumps. He didn't dare straighten up, suddenly mortified by the bulge in his pants. And, wouldn't you know it, He Liping chose that moment to walk along the embankment toward the waterwheel.

Step by step she drew near to Junior, who by then was sitting on the ground. She seemed much bigger all of a sudden, and her hair shimmered with flecks of golden light. Poor Junior's heart was beating like mad, his teeth were chattering. He rested his hands on his knees, and from there let them slide down to the tops of his feet. Finally he scooped little balls of mud out of the ground.

He heard He Liping's voice: "Where's Guo Three?"

He heard his own quaking reply: "He went to Li Gaofa's house."

He heard He Liping walk up to the wooden plank, then heard her spit into the pond. When he looked up to sneak a peek, he found she was leaning over the waterwheel, staring at the gander and duck skimming across the pond. Her rear end stuck up in the air. The sight terrified Junior.

After a while, He Liping asked him how old he was. He told her fifteen. She asked him how come he wasn't in school. He said he didn't want to go.

Junior's face was covered with sweat as he stood in front of He Liping, who started to giggle. He didn't dare raise his head.

Every day after that Guo Three went to Li Gaofa's house to treat the black dog, and He Liping came to pass the time of day with Junior, who was no longer nervous, who no longer broke out in a sweat, who even found the nerve to peek at her once in a while. He could actually smell her.

One very hot day He Liping shed her faded blue tunic, so that she was wearing only a pink undershirt, and when Junior spotted the straps and snaps of her bra he was so happy he nearly wept.

"You little creep," she scolded, "what are you looking at?"

Junior blushed bright red, but still had the courage to say, "I'm looking at your clothes."

With a vinegary frown, she said, "You call these clothes? Wait till you see my nice stuff."

"You look good in anything," Junior said bashfully.

"Quite the little flatterer, aren't we?" He Liping said.

"I've got a skirt," she continued, "that's the same red as those persimmon leaves."

As if on signal, they turned to look at the persimmon tree halfway up the river embankment. After surviving several frosts, the sunlit leaves glowed like bright red flames.

Junior took off running. Halfway up the embankment he climbed the tree and broke off one of the lower branches, which was covered by dozens of glossy red leaves. One had been gnawed by an insect; he plucked it off and threw it away.

The red-leafed branch was a present for He Liping, who sniffed it for its persimmony aroma. Her face was red, maybe a reflection of the leaves.

Guo Three saw Junior give He Liping the red leaves, so

when they were back on the waterwheel, he giggled, "Want me to be your matchmaker?"

Junior blushed to the roots of his ears. "Hell no!"

"Little He isn't bad," Guo Three went on. "Nice perky tits and a good broad beam."

"Don't talk like that," Junior protested. "She's an educated city girl . . . ten years older than me . . . so tall. . . ."

"So what?" Guo Three replied. "Educated girls like doing it as much as anybody. And ten years older, for a girl, is nothing. Besides, 'Tall girl, short boy — tits in the face, what a joy.' Now that's living!"

This little monologue by Guo Three had poor Junior's rear end squirming and his body temperature soaring.

"The little sparrow's standing up," Guo Three remarked. "And not so little, at that."

From that day onward, Guo Three hardly stopped coaching Junior in certain matters, until finally, unable to suppress his curiosity any longer, Junior broached the subject of the "big teapot." Guo Three happily obliged with a graphic description of what went on in a whorehouse.

Junior turned the waterwheel, but his thoughts were miles away: He Liping's image fluttered before his eyes. Guo Three took this as an invitation for even more salacious talk.

With a crack in his voice, Junior pleaded, "Master Three, please don't talk about things like that."

"You dumb prick, what are you getting all weepy about? Go to her. She's itching for it, too!"

So one day Junior went into the production team's vegetable garden and stole a carrot, which he washed off and hid in tall grass until He Liping came along. The oldster Guo Three hadn't arrived when she showed up, so Junior handed her the carrot.

She studied his face as she accepted the gift.

Junior could only imagine what he looked like at that moment, with his matted, grass-stained hair and tattered clothes.

"Why are you giving me this carrot?" He Liping asked him.

"Because I like you," he said.

She sighed and rubbed the carrot's orange, glossy skin. "But you're still a child. . . ." She rubbed his head and walked off with her carrot.

Junior and He Liping went to the distant field to re-sow the millet field. Since draft animals needed room to turn around, some spots were left vacant. They arrived at a field where sorghum had just been harvested. Buds were beginning to appear on the newly planted millet, and dry sorghum stalks were stacked at the head of the patch of ground. It was late autumn by then, and getting cold. After spreading their millet seeds for a while, He Liping and Junior rested in front of a sorghum stack to soak up the warm, inviting rays of sunlight. They had an unobstructed view of the newly harvested and deserted field, over which birds circled noisily.

He Liping laid some bundles of sorghum stalks on the ground and stretched out lazily against them. Junior stood off to the side, gazing down at her. Her face shone in sunlight that was bright enough to make her squint; pretty white teeth showed between her moist, slightly parted lips.

Junior shivered; his lips felt dry, and there was a lump in his throat. "Guo Three and Li Gaofa's wife do you-know-what," he managed to say. "Goes there every day . . ."

Still squinting, He Liping smiled radiantly.

" . . . Guo Three says bad things . . . says you . . ."

Still squinting, He Liping spread her arms and legs wide.

Junior took a step closer. "Guo Three says you're always thinking about doing you-know-what. . . ."

He Liping looked up and smiled.

Junior knelt alongside her. "Guo Three wishes I had the nerve to touch you. . . ."

He Liping was smiling.

Junior began to sob. Through his tears, he said, "Big Sister, I want to touch you . . . want to touch you, Big Sister. . . ."

Junior's hand was no sooner resting upon He Liping's breast than she wrapped her arms and legs tightly around him. . . .

The following year, He Liping gave birth to twins, an event that rocked all of Gaomi Township.

Shen Garden

A THUNDERBOLT CRACKLED ABOVE A LOCUST TREE OUTSIDE THE bakery, sending brilliant sparks flying off a streetcar cable strung beneath the tree. The summer's first clap of thunder caught people out on the street by surprise; they quickly ran for cover under shop overhangs on both sides of the street. Those on bicycles bent low over their handlebars, hugging the sidewalks and pedaling for all they were worth. A cool wind blew amid sheets of rain slanting down. The chaos on the street grew worse as people fled from the downpour.

He and she sat opposite each other at a table in the dark bakery, soft drinks in front of both of them, bright ice cubes bobbing in the dark glasses. Two stale croissants lay on the table, around which a solitary housefly flitted.

He cocked his head to the side to look at the chaotic scene on the street outside. Branches and leaves on the locust tree were buffeted crazily by the wind, which sent fine dust skittering across the ground. The stench of mud filtered into the shop, overwhelming the buttery smell unique to bakeries. Streetcars rolled slowly down the tracks from somewhere off in the distance, nipping at the heels of the ones in front. The heavy rain beating down on the tops of the cars created a cloud of gray mist. The streetcars were packed with passengers, many of whose heads were sticking out of open windows, only to be pelted by stinging drops of rain. The corner of a red dress, caught in one of the streetcar doors, stuck wetly to the step, like a flag of the vanquished.

"Let it pour, the heavier the better," he blurted out through clenched teeth. "It's about time. The city's almost dried up, after six months or more without rain. If this dry spell had lasted much longer, the trees would have withered up and died." He sounded a bit like one of the villains in a revolutionary movie. "How is it there where you are? No rain for a long time, I suspect. I watch the TV weather reports every day to stay on top of your weather there. I was really impressed with that town of yours. I hate big cities, and if not for the kid, I'd have moved there long ago. Small towns are so quiet and cheerful. I wouldn't be surprised if people in your town live ten years longer than those in the cities."

"I'd like to visit Shen Garden," she said.

"Shen Garden?" He turned around to look at her. "Isn't Shen Garden somewhere in Zhejiang Province? Hangzhou? Or maybe Jinhua. You know, the brain's the first to go once you reach middle age. Four or five years ago, I had a terrific memory, but no more."

"I want to visit Shen Garden every time I come to Beijing. But I never get there." Her eyes flashed through the darkness, and her gaunt, pallid face lit up with spirit.

Inwardly shocked by the sight, he turned to avoid her penetrating gaze. He heard himself say hoarsely:

"Here in Beijing we've got Yuanming Gardens and the Summer Palace, but I've never heard of a Shen Garden around here."

She quickly reached down under the seat for her things, put two small plastic bags into a paper shopping bag, and stuffed it into her large plastic handbag.

"Leaving so soon? Aren't you on tonight's eight o'clock train?" Pointing to the croissants, he said casually, "You'd better eat that. You might not get any dinner on the train."

Clutching the plastic handbag to her chest, she stared at him stubbornly and said with downcast insistence:

"I want to visit Shen Garden. I must go see it today."

A gust of cold, rainy wind blew in through the door. He shuddered, rubbing his arms.

"As far as I know, there's no Shen Garden in Beijing. Oh, now I've got it!" he said excitedly. "It's clear now. Shen Garden is way down south in Shaoxing, in Zhejiang Province. I went there once, more than ten years ago. It's not far from the birthplace of Lu Xun. There's a famous carved dialogue between the separated poets Lu You and Tang Wan of the Southern Song dynasty. It goes like this: 'Pink creamy hands/Yellow-labeled wine/Spring colors filling the city/Willows by the palace walls.' If you want the truth, it's a rundown, sort of dreary garden, all covered with weeds. It's like the friend who went with me said, 'You'll be sorry if you miss it, and even sorrier if you see it. . . .'"

By this time she'd stood up and was straightening her clothes. As she smoothed her hair, she said, almost as if she were talking to herself, "This time I'm going to see Shen Garden, no matter what."

Holding up his hand to stop her, he said guardedly, "Okay, let's say Shen Garden is here in Beijing. We'd still have to wait for the rain to let up before we went, wouldn't we? And if you want to go to Shaoxing to see the real Shen Garden, we'll have to wait till tomorrow. There's only one train a day, and today's left hours ago. Airplanes won't fly in this weather, and besides, I don't think there are any direct flights to Shaoxing."

She stepped around his outstretched hand and, still clutching her handbag, walked out the door straight into the downpour. Quickly settling the bill with the two sharp-eyed waitresses, he started after her. Standing in the bakery doorway, he stuck his head outside; the sound of rain beating down on the sheet metal eaves threw his mind into turmoil. He strained to look through the curtain of rain running off the awning like a waterfall and spotted her plastic handbag over her head as she dashed across the street. Taxis speeding past through the puddling rain soaked her skirt, which accentuated the outline of her bony figure. From where he stood under the awning, looking down the street he could see the gray apartment building where he lived and, it seemed, a kaleidoscopic flow of rain coursing down the newly installed sea-blue balcony windows. He even thought he could detect the rich fragrance of brewed tea and the sweet voice of his daughter calling out: "Come here, Papa!"

She stood across from him in the rain, trying to hail a taxi or any car that would stop for her. The blurry outline of her face brought to mind a cold, rainy day nearly twenty years before, when snowflakes swirled in the air: he stood outside the window of her dormitory, looking in at her as she sat in a chair, wearing a white turtleneck sweater, a faint smile on her lovely face as she happily played an accordion. There were times after that when he wanted to tell her about that night, when he'd nearly frozen to death, but he always suppressed the impulse to show his emotions. The young woman playing her accordion seemed to come alive again in the pouring rain, reigniting the remnants of passion deep in his heart.

He rushed out into the rain and across the street to her. In a matter of seconds, he was as drenched as she was, and just as cold. The freezing rain, now mixed with tiny hailstones, felt as if it were boring right through him. Taking her by the arm, he tried to move her over next to one of the commercial buildings, out of the rain, but she resisted, and he gave up trying. His back felt as if it were being pricked by tiny barbs, and when he looked over his shoulder, he saw people under the overhangs casting furtive glances his way. Some of those faces looked familiar. But by then he knew he was stuck. If he let her walk off, his conscience would bother him from that day on.

Finally he managed to drag her over to a roadside telephone booth, where at least the upper halves of their bodies were protected from the rain by a pair of semicircular shades. He said:

"I know of a quaint little Taiwanese teashop in that lane up ahead. Let's go get a nice cup of hot tea and wait for the rain to let up. Then I'll take you to the train station."

The upper half of her body was all but swallowed up by the semicircular shade, so he couldn't see the expression on her face. About all he could see was the dark skirt clinging to her legs to reveal her unattractive, protruding kneecaps. She didn't make a sound, as if his suggestion had fallen on deaf ears. Fewer and fewer cars passed up and down the street, but she kept hailing them, taxis and non-taxis alike, trying to get one of them to stop.

After the rain died down a bit, they finally managed to flag down a red Xiali taxi. He opened the door and let her in first.

Then he climbed in and closed the door. "Where to?" the cabbie asked impassively.

"Shen Garden!" she said before he could answer.

"Shen Garden?" the cabbie replied. "Where's that?"

"Forget Shen Garden," he blurted out. "Take us to Yuanming Gardens."

"No, Shen Garden!" she said in a flat but insistent voice.

"Where is Shen Garden?" the cabbie asked again.

"I said, forget Shen Garden," he repeated. "Take us to Yuanming Gardens."

"Would you make up your minds?" the cabbie said impatiently.

"I told you we want to go to Yuanming Gardens, so take us there." He was beginning to sound shrill.

The cabbie turned back to look at him. He nodded to the gloomy driver. Three times she repeated her desire to go to Shen Garden, but the driver sped down the wide-open street without a response, sending water spraying to both sides. A strange sense of tragic solemnity overcame him as he sat there. Sneaking a look at her, he saw what looked like a pouting smile on her lips. He also noticed that her hand was shaking as she gripped the door handle, as if she were trying to make up her mind to do something rash. He held her right hand tightly to keep her from opening the door and jumping out of the taxi. The hand was cold and clammy, like a dead fish. But it didn't seem as if she wanted to pull it back, since it didn't even twitch. He held it tight, anyway.

The taxi turned onto a narrow street cluttered on both sides with light-colored trash, with the occasional glint of green watermelon rind. Colorful sheets of flypaper draped in front of roadside diners fluttered in the wind and rain. Coarse, dirty women in revealing blouses leaned against doorways, cigarettes dangling from their mouths beneath bored expressions. The sight took his thoughts vaguely back to the town where she lived. "Driver," he said anxiously, "where are we?"

The driver didn't reply. The interior of the taxi was steaming up; the sound of the windshield wipers snapping back and forth was unnerving.

"Where are you taking us?" He was nearly shouting.

"Take it easy!" the driver shot back angrily. "You said you wanted to go to Yuanming Gardens, didn't you?"

"Why are you taking us this way?"

"Which way would you like me to take you?" the driver asked coldly as he slowed down. "Come on, tell me, which way do you want to go?"

"How should I know? But this way seems wrong." Then, softening his tone of voice, he said, "You're the driver, you know the way better than I do."

"I'm glad to hear you say that," the driver replied scornfully. "This is a shortcut. It'll shorten the trip by at least three kilometers."

"Thank you," he said.

"I was going to knock off for the day to go home and get some sleep," the driver said. "Who in his right mind would be out in weather like this? I just felt sorry for you folks. . . ."

"Thank you," he repeated. "Thank you."

"I'm not out to cheat you," the driver said. "Just give me an extra ten yuan. It was your good luck to run into an honest man like me. Now if . . . if you think you're paying too much, get out now and you don't owe me a cent."

As he looked out the window at the gray sky, he said:

"It's only an extra ten yuan, isn't it, driver?"

The taxi sped out of the small street and turned into an even more deserted dirt road with deep muddy puddles. The car raced madly along, splashing water on the roadside trees. The driver was cursing under his breath, either at the road or at the people, hard to tell. Meanwhile, he sat there biting his tongue, his mind filled with ominous premonitions.

The taxi forged its way off the dirt road and onto a gleaming asphalt street. With one last curse, the driver swerved around another corner and screeched to a halt in front of an open gate.

"Is this it?" he asked.

"It's a side entrance. The Western Garden is down the way a bit," the driver said. "I could tell that's what you two wanted to see." He looked down at the meter, added ten yuan to the amount, and handed it through a hole in the wire divider.

"I can't give you a receipt," the driver said.

He ignored him as he opened the door and got out. Then he held the door for her, but she climbed out the other side.

The cabbie turned his car around and drove off. He cursed softly to himself, but once the curse was out, instead of harboring ill thoughts toward the driver, he actually felt grateful to him.

It was still raining. Leaves shone on the roadside trees, clean and incredibly appealing. She stood there in the rain, her face pale as she gazed blankly off into the distance. Taking her by the arm, he said:

"Let's go, dear. Here's your Shen Garden."

Submissively, she let him lead her through the gate into the garden, where peddlers manning stalls along the way shouted out invitingly:

"Umbrellas, umbrellas here. Beautiful, sturdy umbrellas..."

He walked up to one of the stalls and bought two umbrellas, a red one and a black one. Then he walked up to the ticket counter, where he bought a pair of admission tickets. The ticket seller had a large, doughy white face. Her penciled eyebrows looked like two thick green worms.

"What time do you close?" he asked her.

"We never close," doughface replied.

Holding their umbrellas over their heads, they walked into Yuanming Gardens, he in front holding the black umbrella, she following with the red one. The rain beat a steady tattoo on the plastic skins. Clusters or pairs of people passed by in front of them. Some were strolling casually, gaudy umbrellas in hand, while those without umbrellas were scurrying along in the downpour.

"I thought we'd be the only miserable souls...." He regretted the words as soon as they left his mouth. So he quickly changed directions. "But this is special. If it weren't raining so hard, the place would be packed. It always is."

He felt like saying, "Today Yuanming Gardens belong to just you and me." But he caught himself just in time. Together they strolled along the winding path, which glistened like glass. Half-grown lotus leaves and cattails floated on top of the pond off to one side, where frogs leaped along the water's edge.

"Wow, isn't that something!" he shouted excitedly. "Now if only there were a water buffalo grazing by the pond and a flock of white geese gliding on the surface, it would be perfect." Lovingly, he looked at her pale face and said, his voice filled with emotion, "You always sense what's best. If not for you, I'd never have had a chance to see Yuanming Gardens like this."

With a heavy sigh, she said:

"This isn't my Shen Garden."

"You're wrong, this *is* your Shen Garden." He felt like a stage performer. In a tone of voice pregnant with meaning, he added, "Of course, it's *my* Shen Garden too. It's *our* Shen Garden."

"How can you have a Shen Garden?" The sudden sharpness in her eyes made him feel as if he had no place to hide. She shook her head. "Shen Garden is mine, it's mine. Don't you dare try to take it away from me!"

The excitement of a moment before turned to ashes; the scenery around him lost its appeal.

"You're squashing them!" she shrieked in alarm.

Instinctively, he jumped to the side of the path, as she cried out even more shrilly, "You're squashing them!"

When he looked down, he saw an army of tiny jumping frogs. No bigger than soybeans, they were fully formed, little pocket-sized amphibians. Countless numbers of the little things lay squashed on the path, forming perfect outlines of his footprints. She squatted down and moved the little carcasses around with her finger, which was nearly bloodless, with a gray fingernail and an accumulation of dirt. Feelings of disgust, like dregs of filth, welled up from the bottom of his heart.

"Little miss," he said mockingly, "I didn't squash any more than you did. That's right, you didn't squash any fewer than I did. Sure, my feet may be bigger than yours, but you take more steps, so you squashed at least as many as I did."

She stood up and muttered, "That's right, I squashed at

least as many as you did." She wiped her eyes with the back of her hand and said, "Froggies, froggies, how come you're so small?" Then she burst into tears.

"Enough of that, little miss," he said almost jokingly to mask his disgust. "Two-thirds of the people in this world are struggling against deep waters and raging fires, you know!"

She stared at him through her tears.

"They're so small," she said, "but their bodies are perfectly formed!"

"Perfect or not, they're only frogs!" He grabbed her by the arm and pulled her forward. But she threw her umbrella to the ground and, with her free hand, tried to peel his hand away.

"We can't spend the night here all because of a few frogs!" he said angrily as he shook off her hand. But he could see in her eyes that it was futile to try to get her walking again, if she was going to have to squash more frogs in the process. So he picked up her umbrella, took off his shirt, and used it like a broom to shoo the disgusting things off the path ahead. Scattering madly, the little frogs eventually opened up a narrow lane for them. "Hurry up," he said with a tug, "let's go."

Ultimately, they wound up in front of an area covered with rubble. By then the rain had all but stopped and the sky was clearing. After folding their umbrellas, they climbed to the top of a huge boulder that had, sometime in the past, been carefully chiseled by stonemasons. He wrung out his rain-soaked shirt, then shook it out and put it back on. He sneezed, putting as much effort into it as possible to win her sympathy; it didn't work. Shaking his head in mockery of himself, he stood atop the rock and, like all mountain climbers who have reached a summit, thrust out his chest and gulped in the clean air. His mood turned bright and sunny, like the sky, now that the rain had stopped. The air is so clean and fresh here, he was about to remark to her. But he didn't. It was as if they were the only people anywhere in that vast garden, and to him that seemed almost miraculous. Now that he was in a good mood, he took another look at the rubble-strewn ground around him. The huge chiseled rocks were so famous, so evocative, had been framed in so many lenses and shown up in so many poems, yet now they were as common as rocks anywhere. They stood silently, yet somehow seemed to be unburdening themselves of thousands upon thousands of words. They were, in the end, silent stone giants. There in front of the ruins, a pond over which a fountain had sprayed water two centuries earlier was virtually covered by waterweeds, sweet flag, and reeds. Wild grasses he couldn't name flourished in the cracks between rocks.

After helping one another down from the boulder, they went over and climbed another one that was even higher and bigger. Cool winds swept past, slowly drying the clothing that clung to their bodies. The hem of her black skirt began to flutter in the breeze. When he rubbed his hand over the rock, which had been washed clean by the rain, a clean, fresh aroma rose up to greet him. As if a deep, dark secret had been revealed to him, he said:

"Smell this. It's the smell of a rock."

She was gazing fixedly at a stone column that had once supported some large edifice; she looked as if she hadn't heard him. Her gaze seemed capable of boring into the column to discover what was deep inside. At that moment he noticed the strands of gray hair by her temples. A long sigh rose up from the depths of his heart. He reached over and picked up a strand of hair that had fallen to her shoulder and said with heartfelt emotion:

"The time just flies by, and here we are, getting old."

She responded by revealing what was on her mind:

"The words carved on these rocks will never change, will they?"

"Rocks change," he said. "The cliché that seas dry up and rocks rot away, but the heart never changes is nothing but a beautiful fantasy."

"But in Shen Garden nothing ever changes." She was still staring at the rocks, as if conversing with them, while he was reduced to being an inconsequential audience of one. But he was determined to respond to her comment. In a loud voice, he said:

"Not a single thing in this world is eternal. Take this famous garden, for instance. Two hundred years ago, when the Qing emperor built it, no one could have imagined that in the short space of two centuries it would be reduced to ruins. Back then, the marble stones in the vast halls on which the emperor and his ladies took their pleasure might now be the rocks on which commoners have built a pigsty."

Even he sensed how dry and inane his comment was, little more than nonsense. He knew she hadn't heard a word, so he didn't go on. Taking a damp pack of cigarettes out of his pocket, he picked out one that was relatively dry and lit it with his lighter.

A pair of magpies flew past above them and landed on the top of a distant tree, where they chirped noisily. He felt like saying, See how free birds are! But he'd gotten into the habit of swallowing his comments before they broke loose. Just then, a joyous squeal erupted from her mouth and sparks lit up the darkness in her eyes. He cast a surprised look at her, then looked where she was pointing. There in the gray-blue sky was a gorgeous rainbow. She was hopping around like a little girl and shouting at the top of her lungs:

"Look, look!"

Her joy was infectious. The multicolored bridge arching across the sky drove all thoughts of the dark realities of life out of his head, and he was instantly immersed in childlike delights. Without being aware of it, they had drawn close together, as they gazed intimately into each other's eyes. No evasions or sidesteps, no hesitation or wavering; first their hands joined naturally, and then they fell just as naturally into each other's arms. They kissed.

The gorgeous rainbow had disappeared by the time he was sampling the light taste of mud on her lips. The vast ruins spread out around them, a dark purple light glinting off the rocks strewn about and lending a majestic air to the scene. Insects hiding in the waterweeds chirped and clicked, and the crisp honks of geese drifted over from somewhere far off. He glanced casually at her wristwatch. It was seven o'clock.

"Damn!" he blurted out anxiously. "Doesn't your train leave at eight?"

Abandoned Child

I HAD BARELY PICKED HER UP OUT OF THE SUNFLOWER FIELD WHEN I felt that my heart was clogged with gummy black blood and was sinking heavily in my chest, like a cold stone. A grayness filled my head, like a street swept by a cold wind. It was, in the end, her vibrant, croaking wails that roused me out of my bewildered state. I didn't know whether to thank or hate her, and was even less sure whether I was doing a good or a bad thing. I gazed into her long, wrinkled, melon-yellow face with a sense of alarm, seeing two light-green tears in her eyes and the toothless cavern of her mouth — the cries emerging from it were wet and raw, forcing all the blood in my body into my limbs and my head. I could barely hold the red satin-wrapped infant.

I staggered mournfully out of the sunflower field with her in my arms, rustling the leaves shaped like round fans; the white downy hairs on their coarse stems rubbed against my arms and cheeks. I was sweating by the time I emerged from the field; spots on my body that had been scratched by the leaves and stems stood out like red welts from a whip and burned like the stings of insects. But my heart hurt even worse. In the bright sunlight, the satin wrapping of the infant burned my eyes with its fiery redness; it also burned my heart, which felt as if it were enclosed in a layer of ice.

It was high noon; the field spread out around me, the

roadway was a murky gray, and the roadside weeds looked like entwined snakes or worms. A cool wind blew from the west, while the sun's rays blazed, and I couldn't decide whether to complain about the cold or about the heat. It was, in other words, a typical autumn midday. Which meant that the farmers were staying put in their villages.

A little bit of everything grew on one side of the road or the other: soybeans, corn, sorghum, sunflowers, sweet potatoes, cotton, and sesame. The sunflowers were in full bloom, a vast cloud of yellow floating amid the verdant crops. A scant few reddish brown hornets flitted through the subtle fragrance. Crickets set up a mournful cry from beneath the leaves, while locusts flew into the air, only to be snapped up by swallows, some of which perched on low-slung telephone wires stretching over the field. The way their necks were hunched down, I could tell they were eyeballing the smooth gray river that flowed placidly through the field below. I detected a heavy, sticky, life-giving odor like that of raw honey. The vitality of life rose all around me magnificently, and this splendid liveliness manifested itself in a steamy mist rising from the rampant weeds and robust crops. A solitary white cloud hung motionless in the astonishingly blue sky, like a virginal young maiden.

She was crying still, as if she'd been cruelly mistreated. At the time, I didn't know she'd been abandoned. I doubt that my pity, which was worth so little, could prove to be of much benefit to her, but it brought me nothing but agony. I can't help but believe that the saying "good deeds are seldom re-paid in kind" is a law of the universe. You may think yourself virtuous for rescuing someone from the jaws of hell, but others will assume that your actions are self-serving, even destructive! From now on, you won't catch me performing any good deeds. That doesn't mean, of course, that I'll turn to evil. I suffered greatly because of that infant girl, and could feel it coming even as I carried her out of the sunflower field.

I was the only passenger in the rickety bus that had delivered me to the Three Willows stop no more than half an hour before I spotted the baby girl in the sunflower field. During the bus ride I found myself becoming increasingly conscious of the superiority of our social system. The ticket-taker, a girl with a face like a sparrow's egg, was saying the very same thing. The way she yawned all during the trip was a good sign that she hadn't slept the night before — maybe she and her boyfriend had found a more enjoyable way to pass the night. And with each yawn, she turned that lovely face of hers my way and glared at me with such resentment you'd have thought I'd just spat on her or had put powdered lime into her jar of face cream. All of a sudden I had the feeling that dark freckle-like spots covered her eyeballs, and that each time she glared at me, those spots peppered my face like buckshot. I was seized with fear, as if I'd offended her somehow, which was why I greeted each of her looks with the most sincere smile I could manage.

Eventually, she forgave me, for I heard her say, "This is your personal vehicle." Seventeen of the twenty windows in my vehicle, which was some thirty feet long from front to back, were broken, and the black leather seats looked like flat cakes soaked in water, curled up at the edges. My personal vehicle, with all its rusty metal parts, shuddered as it flew down the narrow dirt road, the green fields on both sides quickly disappearing behind us. My personal vehicle was like a warship plowing its way through wind and wave. Without turning to look, my driver asked, "Where are you stationed?" I told him, happily surprised at being favored with his interest. "Is it the fort?" "Yes, yes it is!" Now, I wasn't stationed at the fort, but I knew the benefits of lying — I had been contaminated by a pathological liar. That perked up my driver, and I could see the friendly look on his face even though he hadn't turned around. I must have rekindled a host of memories in him, memories of army life. I echoed his curses, adding my own for the fort's deputy chief of staff, a gangsterlike man with a face like a monkey. He told me he'd once driven for the deputy chief of staff as he sat in back with the wife of the commander of the 38th Regiment. When he looked in the mirror and saw the deputy chief of staff feel the woman up, he'd grimaced and turned the jeep right into a tree . . . ha ha, he laughed. So did I. "I understand," I said, "I understand perfectly. The chief of staff's only human." "When I got back to the fort he told me to fill out a report, so I said, 'I lost my bearings when I saw the deputy chief of staff feel the woman up, and crashed the jeep. It was all my fault.' After I sent it in, our political instructor said 'Fuck you!' and whacked me in the back of the head. 'What kind of report is that? Go back and redo it!'" "Did you?" "No fuckin' way! He wrote it for me, and I copied it." "Your political instructor sounds like a good guy," I said. "Good guy? I had to give him ten fuckin' pounds of cotton!" "Nobody's perfect," I said. "That was during the Cultural Revolution, so it was all the fault of the Gang of Four." "How are things in the army these days?" he asked. "Not bad, not bad at all."

When we arrived in Three Willows, our bus girl opened the door and was about to kick me off the bus. But she didn't scare me, since the driver and I had become comrades in arms. I tossed a pack of Ninety-Nines on the dashboard. That pack of smokes must have made a big hit, since he was still honking his horn in thanks far down the road.

I started walking. I was carrying a sack of candy in my backpack and a small case of liquor in my hand. I'd have to walk the two and a half miles down a country road that never saw a bus, under a blazing sun, before I'd be home with my parents and my wife and daughter. I saw the sunflower field off in the distance. The minute I spotted the note pinned to one of the willow trees, I ran toward it. All because of that note.

Someone had scribbled the words: "In the sunflowers, hurry, save a life!!!"

Suddenly, the sunflower field seemed a long way off, like a cloud floating just above the ground, yellow and soft, its rich fragrance reaching out powerfully to me. I tossed down what I was carrying so I could run faster. And as I ran anxiously, images of something from the past — something I couldn't forget — surged up in my mind. Two summers before, I was walking home, following a white dog, when I ran into a friend I hadn't seen in years, a girl called Aigu. That chance meeting led to a whole string of events, which formed the basis of a short story I later wrote entitled "White Dog and Swings." I still think it's one of my best. Every time I come home, I discover something new, which negates something in the past.

The complex and colorful life of a farming village is like a great work of literature, one that's hard to finish and even harder to understand. That thought always reminds me of the shallow, insipid business of writing. What strange new discovery was waiting for me this time? If the note I'd read was any indication, it was bound to be "exciting" and "tragic," to use terminology favored by elite writers. Yuri and Lara carried out their trysts amid sunflowers, a warm and romantic Eden just made for losing your senses. I was nearly breathless when I reached the edge of the field. The coarse sunflower leaves were rustling in the warm breezes; dragonflies, crickets, and katydids were making their happy yet bleak noises; and then the baby girl who would bring me unimaginable troubles began to wail. Her cries were the lead instrument in the sunflower symphony — fast and anxious, urgent as a flame singeing the eyebrows.

I'd never seen an entire field of sunflowers before. I was used to seeing clumps or thickets of them by a bamboo fence or at the base of a wall; there they stood tall but lonely, almost as if they were humiliated. But a field of sunflowers stood side by side, gently and intimately supporting each other, resembling a sea of undulating passion. The expansion of sunflowers, from clusters here and there to an entire field, was a heartwarming reflection of the effects of economic reforms in agricultural villages.

It would be several days before I fully realized that this baby girl, abandoned in a lovely field of sunflowers, was a strange creature, the focus of so many contradictions that it would have been unthinkable to abandon her and just as unthinkable to keep her. Mankind has evolved to the point where all that separates it from the animal world is a line as thin as a sheet of paper. Human nature is in fact as thin and fragile as a sheet of paper, which crumples at the slightest touch.

The thick sunflower stems were gray green; their bottom leaves had already fallen, leaving tiny scars where they had broken off, while those higher up blocked out the light. The leaves were dark green, nearly black, and lusterless. Countless flowers the size of rice bowls dipped gently atop the stems, like a multitude of bowing heads. I followed the sounds into the field, sending clouds of golden pollen fluttering down onto my hair and arms, even into my eyes; fluttering down to the rain-leveled ground; fluttering down onto the infant's red satin wrapping; and fluttering down on three pagoda-like anthills near where she lay. Hordes of black ants caught up in a flurry of activity were intent on building their stronghold. Bone-corroding despair hit me all of a sudden. Besides helping humans forecast the weather, the ants' frenetic industry was absolutely worthless, for their hills could barely withstand thirty seconds of pelting rain. Given man's place in the universe, how superior to those ants are we? Terror exists everywhere you look: we are surrounded by traps, by deceit and by lies and self-serving corruption; even fields of sunflowers are places to hide red infants. I thought about leaving her where she lay, turning around, and continuing on my way home, but I couldn't do it. It was as if she were welded to my arms. Time and again I decided to leave her there, but my arms had a mind of their own.

I walked back to Three Willows to study the note again. The scribbled words stared back at me savagely. The surrounding field was vast as ever; autumn cicadas on their last legs chirped desolately in the willow trees, and the winding dirt road leading to the county capital emitted a blinding yellow glare. A scruffy cat, banished from its home, slipped out from a cornfield, looked at me, and meowed once before creeping listlessly into a patch of sesame.

After looking down at the infant's puffy, nearly transparent lips, I picked up my backpack and box and, cradling her in my arms, headed for home.

My family was happily surprised to see me appear out of the blue, but they were positively astonished to see the infant in my arms. Father and Mother showed their astonishment by tottering slightly on their feet; my wife showed hers by letting her arms drop to her side. Only my five-year-old daughter displayed any excitement toward the infant, and that was considerable. "A baby brother!" she shouted. "A baby brother! Papa's brought home a baby brother!"

I knew that my daughter's intense interest in a "baby brother" was born of long coaching by my parents and my wife. Every time I came home, she'd pester me for a baby brother — not just one, in fact, but two of them. And each time that happened, I could sense the somber yet gentle looks in the eyes of my parents and my wife as they gazed at me hopefully, as if I were on trial.

On one occasion, I'd fearfully taken a pink male doll out of my travel bag and handed it to my daughter while she was creating one of her scenes over a baby brother. She'd taken it from me and immediately hit it in the head, producing a resounding thud. Then she'd flung it to the floor and begun to bawl. "I don't want that," she said through her tears. "This one's dead . . . I want a baby brother who can talk." After picking the plastic toy up off the floor, I'd looked into its protruding eyes and seen a look of uncommon ridicule. All I could do was sigh. Father and Mother had also sighed. Then I'd looked up and there was my wife, two lines of murky tears coursing down the lacquerlike skin of her dark face.

Except for my daughter, they all looked at me with numb expressions, which I returned to them. I smiled bitterly to ease my discomfort, and they followed suit, not making a sound. They all wore the same molten look on their taut faces, as if etched into clay figurines.

"Papa, let me see my baby brother!" my daughter shouted as she jumped up and down.

"I found it," I announced. "In the sunflower field . . ."

My wife reacted angrily: "I can still have babies!"

"Do you expect me to turn my back on a child in danger?" I asked her in a pleading tone.

"You did the right thing," Mother said. "You couldn't walk away."

Father didn't say a word the whole time.

As I laid the baby down on the bed, fitful wails erupted.

I said it was hungry. My wife glared at me.

"Unwrap it and let's see what the baby looks like," Mother volunteered.

Father laughed coldly and squatted down on the floor, taking out his tobacco pouch; soon he was puffing away at his pipe.

My wife moved quickly up to the bed and untied the cloth band holding the satin wrap together. One brief glance and she backed away despondently.

"Let me see Baby Brother!" my daughter cried out as she pushed up and put her hands on the edge of the bed, trying to climb up. "Let me see him!"

My wife bent over and pinched her hard on the backside.

With a loud shriek, our daughter ran out into the compound and cried at the top of her lungs.

It was a little girl. Kicking her blood-spattered, wrinkled legs, she wailed piteously. Her arms and legs were in good shape, her features looked just right, and her cries were nice and loud. No mistake about it, she was a fine little baby. A pile of black excrement lay under her backside; I knew this was what they call "fetal feces." Which meant that the squirming little object lying softly in the red satin was a newborn infant.

"It's a girl!" Mother said.

"If it wasn't, who would be willing to throw it away?" Father said darkly as he banged the bowl of his pipe on the floor.

My daughter sounded as if she were singing a song out in the yard, but she was still crying.

"You can just take it back where you found it," my wife said.

"That would be the same as leaving it to die," I protested. "This is a human life we're talking about, so don't try turning me into a criminal."

"Let's take care of her for the time being," Mother said, "while we ask around to see if anyone is missing a child. You need to go all the way in things like this. It's like seeing a parting guest to his door. This good deed will ensure that your next pregnancy will produce a son."

Mother, no, everyone in the family, was hoping against hope that my wife and I would produce a son so I could fulfill my responsibilities as a son and a husband. It had become such a powerful demand, accompanying my wife and me without letup over the years, that you could cut the tension with a knife. It was a noxious desire that had begun to poison the mood of everyone in the family; the looks in their eyes tore at my soul like steelyard hooks. Time and again I was on the verge of laying down my arms and surrendering, but I always stopped myself. It had reached the point where anytime I was out walking, I was gripped by a deep-seated terror. People kept giving me funny looks, as if I were a mental case or a strange creature from some alien planet who had landed in their midst. I cast a sad glance at my mother, whose devotion to my well-being knew no bounds. By then I didn't even have the strength to sigh.

I picked up a scrap of toilet paper to clean the baby's bottom. Hordes of flies, attracted by the smell, swarmed over from the toilet, the pigsty, and the cattle pen, forming a nasty black tide as they buzzed around the room. Masses of bedbugs leaped up out of the darkness beneath the bed, as if shot from a gun. The fetal feces was hard and sticky, like softened pitch or a warmed medicinal plaster; it smelled awful. A mild sense of disgust rose in me as I cleaned it up.

My wife, who had by then gone into the outer room, came back and said, "The way you ignore your own kid, it's as if you're not her real father. But you'll even wipe the butt of somebody else's kid, like she was your own flesh and blood. Who knows, maybe she is. Maybe she belongs to you and some woman out there. Maybe you went out and had yourself a nice little daughter . . ."

Her grumbling merged with the infernal buzzing of the flies, nearly liquefying my brain. "Knock it off!" I shouted hysterically.

That shut her up. I stared at her face, which, out of rage and fear, had undergone a dramatic change. I could also hear my daughter, who was playing with a neighbor girl somewhere in the lane. Girls, girls, unwelcome girls everywhere.

Despite all my care, some of the fetal feces soiled my hand. There was something wonderful, I felt, about cleaning up an abandoned baby's first bowel movement. Feeling honored, I went back to cleaning her up, scooping out the dark excrement with my finger. Out of the corner of my eye, I looked at my wife, whose mouth hung slack, and at that moment, a sense of deep-rooted loathing for all of humanity exploded inside me. Naturally, self-loathing topped the list.

My wife came up to help. I neither welcomed her help nor rejected it. When she reached down and expertly straightened the swaddling cloth, I stepped back, scooped up some water, and washed the excrement off my hand.

"Money!" my wife cried out.

I held up my hands, turned, and saw her holding a loose piece of red paper in her left hand and a wad of crumpled bills in her right. She let go of the red paper, spit once, and began counting. She did it twice, just to make sure. "Twenty-one yuan!" Her face exuded tenderness.

"Go get Shasha's baby bottles," I said, "and wash them. Then fill one with powdered milk and feed the baby."

"Are you serious about taking her in?" she asked.

"We'll worry about that later," I said. "For now we don't want her to starve."

"There's no powdered milk in the house."

"Then go buy some at the co-op!" I took out ten yuan and handed it to her.

"We're not using our own money," she said, waving the dirty bills in her hand. "We'll use her money."

A cricket bounded out from a corner of the damp wall and landed on the edge of the bed, then crawled over the red wrapping. The insect's coffee-colored body looked especially somber against the deep red of the satin. I saw its antennae twitch nervously. The baby stuffed one of her hands into her mouth and began to suck. The white skin over her knuckles was peeling. She had a full head of black hair and two big, fleshy, nearly transparent ears.

Just when, I don't know, but my father and mother had moved up beside me and were watching the hungry baby chew her fist.

"She's hungry," Mother said.

"People have to learn how to do everything but eat," Father said.

I turned to look at the two old folks, and waves of heat rolled up from my heart. As if they were praying to the Holy Ghost, they stood with me admiring the dirty, bloodstained face of a girl who might someday become a great woman.

My wife returned with two sacks of powdered milk and a package of detergent. I mixed a bottle of milk, then shoved the plastic nipple, which my daughter had nearly chewed to pieces, into the baby's mouth. The baby rocked its head back and forth a time or two before wrapping her lips around the nipple and beginning to gurgle.

After finishing the bottle, she opened her eyes. They were black as tadpoles. She struggled to look at me, but her gaze was cold and detached.

"She's looking at me," I said.

"A newborn baby can't see anything," Mother said.

"How do you know what she can and can't see?" Father objected angrily. "Did she call you up and tell you?"

Mother backed away. "I'm not going to argue with you. I don't care if she can see or not."

Just then our daughter ran in from the lane and shouted, "Mother, did you hear that thunder? It's going to rain."

She was right. From where we were standing inside the house, we could hear peals of thunder rolling in from the northwest, like the sound of a millstone turning. I saw dark, downy clouds through holes poked in the paper covering of the rear window.

Shortly after noon, the skies opened up, and a gray curtain of rain sluiced down from the tile overhangs, the sound merging with the croaking of frogs. A dozen or more huge carp shaped like plow blades had been carried along by the river of rainwater and were now flopping around in the yard. My wife was fast asleep in bed, holding our daughter in her arms; I could hear my parents' heavy breathing in their bed in the other room. After placing the baby girl in a bamboo winnowing basket, I carried it into the front room and set it down on a tall stool, then sat down beside her and gazed out at the wild torrents of rain falling outside. When I turned back to look at the baby, she was curled up in the basket, sleeping soundly. The rain sheeted down off the eaves onto an upturned bucket, the sound shifting from a crisp pelt to an urgent dull pounding. What little light entered the room from the leaden skies was a dark blue, turning the baby's face the color of orange peel. Worried that she would wake up hungry, I held a bottle of milk in readiness, as if it were a fire extinguisher, just in case. Every time she opened her mouth to cry, I stuffed the nipple in it, stopping the crying before it had a chance to blossom. Not until I noticed milk seeping out of the sides of her mouth did I come to my senses: the baby could die from too much to eat as easily as she could starve. I stopped feeding her and cleaned the milk out of her eyes and ears with a towel, then turned again to look anxiously at the steady rain. It was already obvious that this baby had become a burden, my burden. If not for her, I'd have been in bed by then, sleeping off the fatigue from my long bus ride. Instead, because of her, I was sitting on a hard stool, watching the numbing rainfall outside. If not for me, by then she might already have drowned, either that or frozen to death. She could have been swept along into a trough by the gush of rainwater, to have her eyes pecked at by hungry fish.

One of the marooned carp lay on the path in the yard, belly up, its tail flapping against the tiles, a muted glare emerging from it. Finally it flipped back into the puddling water. When it stretched out straight, it looked like a plow knifing through the water. I was tempted to run out in the rain and scoop it up for a treat for Father, something to go with his wine. But I held back, and not just because I wanted to avoid getting soaked.

That afternoon, with rain falling like darts, I suffered the onslaught of mosquitoes as I pondered my hometown's history of abandoned children. Without having to consult any written material, I had a clear historical sense of children who had been given up by parents in my hometown. Relying solely upon the

keen bite of memory, I chewed open up a dim tunnel through
the sealed history of local abandoned children. Heading down
that path, I kept bumping up against their cold, white bones.

I grouped the children into four general categories, knowing full well that there was unavoidable overlap.

The first group of children included those abandoned by
families mired in poverty; unable to raise the children, they
drowned them in chamber pots or simply left them by the side
of the road. Most of these cases occurred before the founding
of the People's Republic, when family planning was unheard
of. This sort of abandonment appears to be a worldwide phenomenon. I was reminded of two Japanese stories. One, entitled "Snow Babies," was written by Minakami Tsutomu; I can't
recall who wrote the second one, entitled "Dolls of Michinoku," but maybe it was the famous author of *The Ballad of
Narayama*. Both works deal with abandoned children. In
"Snow Babies," the children are left in the snow to die, but
those whose will to live is strong enough to carry them through
the night in their snowy tombs are retrieved by their families
and taken home. As for the babies of Michinoku, before they
even cut loose with their first wail, they are dumped headfirst
into a vat of hot water. People back then believed that babies
had no feelings until they drew their first breath, and that
drowning them then was not an inhuman act. If the babies
managed to cry, their parents were obliged to raise them. Both
means of abandonment were known in my hometown, and
their causes were as I stated earlier — my groupings were
based upon causes. I was confident that over the years a great
many local babies had died in chamber pots, in dirtier and far
crueler fashion than their Japanese counterparts. Of course,

even if I'd asked all the local elders, none of them would have owned up to such infanticide. Yet I recalled the looks on their faces as they sat by wattle fences or at the base of a broken wall; to me those were the looks of baby killers, and I was sure that some of them had ended the lives of their own sons or daughters in chamber pots or by leaving them by the sides of roads to starve or freeze to death. They were children no one bothered to save. To these people, leaving children by the side of a road or at an intersection was somehow more humane than drowning them in a chamber pot; in fact, this was nothing more than self-consolation by decent fathers and mothers in the grip of poverty. Put out to die, these children had an incredibly slim chance of living, and most probably ended up filling the rumbling stomachs of wild dogs.

The second group of abandoned children includes those born with disabilities or who are retarded. These children aren't even entitled to end up in a chamber pot. In most cases, the parents bury the child alive in some remote spot before the sun comes up. They then top the burial mound with a brick directly over the infant's abdomen, to keep it from being reborn during the next pregnancy. But this is not always carried out. Shortly after Liberation, Li Manzi, who is now a local district chief, was born with a harelip.

Illegitimate children comprise the third group of abandoned babies. "Illegitimate" is a powerful insult for anyone, and in my hometown, anytime a young woman gets particularly angry at someone, this is what she calls them. An illegitimate child, of course, is one born to an unmarried woman. Most of these children are bright and attractive, because men and women who are adept at sneaking around to produce a love child are nobody's fools. These offspring have a somewhat higher survival rate, since childless couples are often willing to raise them as their own; often they'll arrange to take them in beforehand, and once they're born, their biological fathers deliver them to their adoptive parents in the dead of night. Others are left someplace where they're easily spotted. And most of the time, money or valuables are tucked into the swaddling cloth. This group of abandoned children often includes boys, while there are seldom any boys in the previous two categories, except for those who are disabled.

The period after Liberation, owing to improvements in living standards and hygiene, saw a significant drop in the occurrences of abandoned children. But the numbers began to rise again in the 1980s, when the situation grew very complicated. First, there were no boys at all. On the surface, it appeared that some parents were forced into acts of inhumanity by rigid family planning restrictions. But upon closer examination, I realized that the traditional preference for boys over girls was the real culprit. I knew I couldn't be overly critical of parents in this new era, and I also knew that if I were a peasant, I might well be one of those fathers who abandoned his child.

No matter how much this concept tarnishes the image of the People's Republic, it is an objective reality, one that will be difficult to eradicate in the short term. Existing in a filthy village with foul air all around, even a diamond-studded sword will rust. So, it seems, I awakened to the Truth.

All night long it rained, but as dawn broke, a ray of sunlight — blood-red, wet and hot — split the dark clouds. I carried the baby over to the bed and asked my wife to watch her. Then I went outside to slosh through the muddy puddles of rainwater and to cross the river on my way to the township government office to ask for help. As I entered the lane, I saw that the sorghum stalk fence had been blown down by gusty winds, leaving lush morning glories to soak in the water. Purple and pink blossoms had turned to face the clearing sky, as if offering a sorrowful complaint. Now that the collapsed fence was no longer a barrier, a clutch of half-grown chickens, their feathers still growing, rushed into the yard to peck frantically at large heads of cabbage.

The river's floodwater all but submerged the little stone bridge, sending spray high into the air when it crashed against the stones. I twisted my ankle when I jumped off the bridge, and as I hobbled along the dike, I couldn't help but think that this was not a good sign, that this trip to the township office might not solve my problem. But I kept hobbling as best I could toward the row of tiled buildings.

Rain had washed the government compound until everything was clean and fresh. Red bricks and green tiles, and the surrounding thickets of green bamboo, sparkled wetly. There were no human sounds in the compound. A pointy-eared mongrel watchdog with a missing tail lay on the concrete steps staring at me warily, before narrowing its eyes. A check of wooden signs above a series of doors led me to the office I was looking for. I knocked — three times. Suddenly I heard a rustling behind me, just before I felt a sharp pain in my leg. I looked down, but by then the damned watchdog, which had just bitten me on the calf, had already returned to the step and was sprawled out lazily. It didn't make a sound as it lay there licking its chops; it even flashed me a friendly smile. How could I help but feel a fondness for a dog like that, even though it had just bitten me? You might think I'd hate it, but I didn't hate it. In my view, it was one terrific dog. But why had it bitten me? It was not a random act, so there must have been a reason. In this world, there is no love without reason or cause; nor, for that matter, hatred. Most likely the bite was intended for me to reach a sudden awakening through pain. True danger never comes from the front, always from the rear; true danger is not embodied in a mad dog with bared fangs, but in the sweet smile of, say, a Mona Lisa. I'd have missed that fact if I'd not been forced to think about it; once the thought struck me, I was startled into awareness. Thank you, dog, you with the pointy snout and a face drenched in artistic colors!

My pant leg felt sticky, and hot. That must have meant blood. Anytime I bled for someone, the person who'd drunk my blood would curse me, "Your blood is rancid! Get the hell out of here!" I wondered if this abandoned child I'd rescued might also curse me for having rancid blood.

The door, whose green paint had begun to peel and chip, was flung open, and there in front of me stood a dark-skinned mountain of a man. After sizing me up, he demanded, "Who are you looking for?"

"The Township Head," I said.

"That's me. Come in, have a seat. Hey, your leg's bleeding. How'd that happen?"

"Your dog bit me."

The dark-skinned man's face twisted into anger. "Damn! Would you look at that! I'm sorry. It's all Scarface Su's fault. The People's Compound isn't some landlord's mansion, so why keep a watchdog around? Is that a hint that the People's Government is afraid of the people? Or that we're in favor of having vicious dogs rupture the flesh-and-blood ties with the people?"

"That doesn't rupture ties," I said, pointing to my injured leg, "it molds them."

By then the blood had dripped from my calf down to the heel of my shoe, and from there to the brick floor, where it was soaked up by a long cigarette butt. I saw the brand name — it was Front Gate, the tobacco strips the color of yellow chrysanthemums.

"Little Wang!" the dark-skinned man shouted. "Come in here!" The man rushed into the room and stood with his arms at his sides, waiting for instructions. "Take this comrade soldier over to the clinic for treatment," the dark-skinned man said. "And bring a receipt back for reimbursement. Then go borrow a rifle from Supply Department Head Xia, and shoot that damned dog!"

I stood up. "Chief, that's not why I'm here to see you," I said. "I want to report something important. I can take care of the injury to my leg myself, and I'd rather you let the dog live. He's quite a dog, and I'm in his debt."

"I don't care. We were going to have to shoot that dog sooner or later anyway! It's a menace! You couldn't know, but it's already bitten twenty people! You're the twenty-first. If we don't put the thing down now, it might really hurt somebody someday. There's enough chaos around here already. We don't need any more."

"Please don't kill it, Chief," I said. "It's got its reasons for biting people."

"All right," the dark-skinned man said with a wave of his hand, "all right. What is it you want to see me about?"

I fumbled in my pocket for a cigarette, which I handed to him. "I don't smoke," he said with an emphatic wave.

Somewhat embarrassed, I lit one for myself and stammered, "Chief, I found an abandoned girl."

His eyes lit up like torches; he snorted.

"It was yesterday, about noon, in the sunflower field east of Three Willows. A girl, wrapped in red satin, along with twenty-one yuan."

"Here we go again!" he blurted out, annoyed.

"I couldn't just let her die!" I said.

"Did I say you should have? What I said was, here we go again! Here we go again! You have no idea of the pressure I'm under. Once the peasants got their land, they saw themselves as free men, who were also free to have as many kids as they wanted. One after another, that's all they did, at least until they got the sons they wanted."

"Don't we have a one-child policy?"

He smiled a wry smile. "One child? Two kids, three kids, four, even five, I've seen it all. One-point-one billion people? That's a laugh. I'll bet we're up to one-point-two by now. There isn't a township anywhere that doesn't have at least two or three hundred unregistered kids. And they'll all rot right here in China!"

"I thought they could be fined."

"That's right. Two thousand for the second child, four thousand for the third, and eight thousand for the fourth. And so what? People with money don't care if you fine them. You're from East Village, aren't you? Do you know Two-Toothed Wu? He's got four kids. No land, a run-down three-room house, one big cook pot, a water jug, and a rickety three-legged table. So we fine him, and he says, 'I don't have any money, so I'll give you kids instead. You want one? Take one. You want two? Take two. They're all girls anyway.' So tell me, what are we supposed to do?"

"Forced sterilizations . . . hasn't that been done?" I asked cautiously.

"It sure has. It's the hottest policy these days. But those people can smell us out better than a hound dog. As soon as they're tipped off, they light out for the northeast, where they cool their heels for a year. By the time they're back in the spring, they've got another kid to raise. If I had access to reinforcements, shit, I'd be in fine shape! Pricks that'll do stuff like that aren't human. I don't dare go out walking at night anymore. I'm afraid of getting mugged."

My dog-bit leg twitched.

He laughed contemptuously.

I could see the hound dog through the open door; it was sprawled comfortably and, apparently, safely on the steps. Department Head Xia of the Supply Department probably didn't have a gun at his house.

"What about the girl I found?"

"There's nothing I can do," the dark-skinned man said. "You found her, so she's yours. Take her home and raise her."

"What kind of attitude is that, Chief? She's not mine, so why should I raise her?"

"You don't expect me to raise her, do you? The Township Government isn't an orphanage."

"Not me, I can't raise her."

"Then what do you suggest? The government didn't force you to take the kid home."

"Then I'll put her back where I found her."

"That's up to you. But if she starves to death in the sunflower field, or is torn apart by dogs, you'll be charged with infanticide."

I choked, then coughed as tears welled up in my eyes.

He looked at me sympathetically and poured some tea in a glass coated with half an inch of crud. I sipped the tea and gazed at him.

"Go ask around," he said. "Maybe there's a widow or widower somewhere who's willing to take in a child. If not, then just take her home and raise her yourself. Do you have family in the village? Including a child? If so, and you take this one into your home, that'll make two kids. We'll have to fine you two thousand."

"Damn you!" I jerked my glass of tea up into the air, but then laid it down gently. With tears clouding my eyes, I said, "Tell me, Chief, does justice exist anywhere in this world?"

He just grinned, showing his strong, yellow front teeth.

My leg itched terribly, and when I saw drops of liquid on the floor, I shuddered. I figured it had to be rabies. Even my gums began to itch, and I had a powerful urge to bite somebody. From behind me, the dark-skinned man said, "Don't worry, somebody will take her. And we'll help any way we can."

All I wanted to do was take a bite out of him!

Six days passed. The baby went through the sack of powdered milk, had six healthy bowel movements, and peed a dozen or more times into four diapers I'd begged from my wife, changing them as often as necessary. I must say that she was reluctant to "lend" me the diapers, since she was saving them for our future son. After washing and folding them neatly, she'd stacked them in a chest like handkerchiefs. She did not hide the look of deep disapproval when she handed them to me.

The baby had an enviable appetite and a strong pair of lungs, as her cries proved. She didn't seem at all like a newborn baby. I hunkered down next to her as she lay in the winnowing basket and fed her from the bottle, gripped by a gray chill as I watched her swallow the nipple and observed the fierce look on her face when she gulped the milk down in a frenzy. She frightened me, for I sensed that she presented a constellation of calamities for me. I often asked myself why I'd picked her up in the first place. My wife took pleasure in reminding me that her own parents hadn't given a damn about her, so why should I be the do-gooder? Squatting down beside the winnowing basket, I was often taken back to that sun-drenched field of sunflowers, where flowery heads drooped of their own weight to roll mechanically and clumsily around the stalks, sending so much fine golden pollen raining to the ground like teardrops that it even swamped anthills.

My nose told me that the skin around the dog bite had begun to rot; flies were already circling the infected area, their bellies packed with microscopic maggots, like a fully loaded bomber. I figured the infection would probably spread until the whole rotten limb was stiff as a frozen gourd. I wondered what this little girl would think of me after the leg was amputated and I had to walk with crutches, lurching back and forth like the pendulum of a clock. Would she be as grateful to me as ever? No way. Not on your life. Any time I made a major sacrifice for anyone, all I ever got in return was deep-seated loathing and vicious curses, unparalleled in their savagery. My heart was deeply scarred, pierced all the way through. And whenever I offered it to someone, fully marinated in soy sauce, all they ever did was piss on it. I loathed humanity, in all its hideousness, from the depths of my soul, and that included this gluttonous baby girl. Why had I rescued her in the first place? I could hear her reproachful voice: Why did you rescue me? Did you expect gratitude? If not for you, I'd have long since departed this filthy world, you perverse blundering fool! What you deserve is another dog bite.

As my thoughts ran wild, my attention was caught by a mature smile creasing the baby's face, sweet as beet sugar. She had a tiny dimple, the skin between her eyebrows had begun to flake, and her elongated head had gotten rounder. No matter how you looked at it, she was a lovely, healthy baby. In the face of this warm, sincere life, splendid as a sunflower — there I was, thinking about sunflowers again — I refuted all my absurd thoughts. Maybe I was wrong to loathe people, and now it was time to love them. The philosophy teacher reminded me that pure hate and pure love are both ephemeral and should coexist. So be it: I would loathe and love people at the same time.

The twenty-one yuan I'd found in the swaddling clothes had barely paid for one sack of milk powder, and I'd made no progress in my search for a new home. My wife's constant mutterings rang in my ears. And my parents, well, they were like marionettes, often going the whole day without saying a word, a perfect complement to my gabby wife. Our daughter was fascinated by the new baby, often sitting beside me as I squatted by the winnowing basket and stared at the little girl lying inside it. Anyone seeing us might have thought we were captivated by some strange tropical fish.

If I couldn't find somewhere to dispose of the baby very soon, and if she ate up the twenty-one yuan her parents had left with her, I knew what was in store for me. So off I went, dragging my injured leg behind me as I visited every one of the dozen or more villages in the township, begging for help from every childless family. The answer was virtually the same every time: We want a son, not a daughter. Up till then, I had always considered my township to be a special place with upstanding people, but a few days of traveling from one end to the other quickly changed that opinion. The place was teeming with ugly little boys, all of whom stared at me with eyes like dead fish, deep wrinkles creasing their foreheads, the expressions on their faces those of long-suffering, hateful impoverished peasants. They shuffled along when they walked, their backs were already stooped, and they coughed like old men. The sight intensified my sense that mankind was in worse shape than ever. To me, they were living proof that the villages in my township were filled with "little treasures" who should never have been born in the first place. Despairing for the future of my hometown, I forced myself not to think of the posterity these males who were old before their time might produce.

One day, while I was out on the road trying to unload the baby, I ran into an old friend from elementary school. He couldn't have been more than twenty-two or twenty-three, but he looked fifty. When the conversation turned to families, he said sadly, "I'm still a bachelor, and I guess that's how I'll stay."

"I thought you were well off financially."

"I'm doing all right, but there just aren't enough women to go around. If I had sisters, I could work a swap for a wife. Unfortunately, I don't."

"I thought township regulations outlawed that kind of marriage arrangement."

He gave me a puzzled look. "Just what do those township regulations mean?"

I nodded. When I told him about the baby I'd found and all the trouble that had caused me, he listened in stony silence, without a trace of sympathy in his eyes. He just puffed on the cigarette I'd given him. The tip of the cigarette sizzled, but not a wisp of smoke emerged from his mouth or nose. As far as I could tell, it all disappeared deep down in his stomach.

Five days later he came to see me. With obvious embarrassment, he said, "Why not . . . why not give me the baby? I'll raise her till she's eighteen. . . ."

I looked agonizingly into his face, which showed even greater agony, waiting for him to continue.

"When she's eighteen . . . I'll only be fifty . . . and who says I can't . . ."

"Old friend," I interrupted, "don't say any more, please."

I bought two more sacks of powdered milk with my own money, to which my wife responded by smashing one of our chipped bowls. Through tears of genuine sorrow, she said, "I've had it! I can't take it anymore! You obviously don't care what happens to us anyway. . . . I've scrimped on food till I don't need to go to the toilet anymore, just to save money. And for what? So you can buy milk for somebody else's kid?"

"You're my wife," I said, "so please don't take your unhappiness out on me. You see me go out every day to find a home for her, don't you?"

"You should never have brought her home in the first place."

"Yes, I know that. But I did, and we can't let her starve."

"What does that make you, a man with a good heart?"

"Good people don't get what they deserve, do they? After all these years we've been together, I wish you wouldn't nag me. If you've got a solution, tell me, what is it? We can work together to place this child somewhere, what do you say?"

"Yes," she said, flashing her most fetching pout. "Once we get rid of this child, we can have another one of our own."

"Have another one?"

"Yes, a son!"

"Another one!"

"Twins would be best."

"Yes. Yes."

"Go to the hospital and talk to our aunt. Maybe she can come up with something. Widows and widowers from the city are always asking her to help them find children."

The final battle. If my aunt, who worked in the hospital's obstetrics ward, couldn't help me find a home, the chances were 80 or 90 percent that I was fated to be the baby's adoptive father. If that's how this all wound up, it would be an unending calamity both for her and for me. I lay in bed that night, oblivious to the onslaught of bedbugs, listening to my wife grind her teeth, smack her lips, and breathe heavily as she dreamt; my heart felt as if it had turned to ice. Finally, I crawled quietly out of bed and went outside, where I looked up at the desolate stars in the sky and felt I had, at last, found a bit of understanding. The damp night air wet my back, and my nose ached from sadness. All of a sudden I knew the importance of treasuring my own life; for too long I'd lived for other people, and vowed to reserve some of the love in my soul for myself. Back inside, I heard the gentle, even breathing of the baby in her winnowing basket. Picking up a flashlight, I shone it down on her. She'd wet herself again, and the liquid had seeped through the slats of the basket onto the floor. I changed her diaper. With Heaven's help, this would be the last time I had to do that!

My aunt, who had just finished delivering a baby, was sprawled in a chair in her white uniform, which was covered with sweat and drops of blood, trying to catch her breath. She'd gotten a lot older in the year since I'd last seen her. She bent forward in greeting when she saw me walk in. Her nurse was in the delivery room cleaning up; a newborn infant in its cradle was bawling.

I sat down in the same nurse's chair I'd sat in the year before, directly across from my aunt. A plastic-covered obstetrics textbook for nurses lay on the table.

"What are you doing back here?" she asked lazily. "After you were here last year, you went back and wrote a book that made me look like some kind of demon!"

"It wasn't well written," I said with an embarrassed smile.

"Want to hear a story about a fox fairy?" she asked. "If I'd known that even a fox fairy tale could wind up in a book, I'd have given you a whole trainful of them."

Without any encouragement from me, and no regard for how exhausted she was after having delivered a baby, she told me a story. During the previous winter, she began, an old man out gathering manure early one morning encountered a fox with a broken leg. He picked it up and carried it home on his back as a pet. The fox's injured leg was nearly healed when the old man's son came to visit. This son, an impetuous young fellow, was a battalion commander. The moment he laid eyes on the fox, he took out his revolver and, without a word, shot it dead. As if that weren't enough, he skinned the animal and nailed its hide to the wall to dry out. The old man nearly died of fright, but his son merely hummed a little tune, unfazed by what he'd done.

At noon the next day, the old man's son made fox dumplings for lunch: he sliced the meat; chopped up coriander, leeks, and onions; and added sesame oil, soy sauce, pepper, and MSG — a cornucopia of flavors. The skins he fashioned out of turnip flour — white and shiny, like pieces of fine ceramic. When they were all wrapped, he dumped them into a pot of boiling water — once, twice, three times, until they were ready to eat. But when he scooped them out, all that came up were little donkey turds. He scooped up some more. More donkey turds. And again, with the same result. The son's hair stood on end. That night, when every door and window in the house began to rattle, the son took out his revolver; but nothing happened when he pulled the trigger. Finally, they had no choice but to perform funeral rites for the fox.

My aunt knew so many fox and ghost stories it would have taken her three days and nights to tell them all, and since the time, place, and other details were based on fact, you had to believe them. Her talents were wasted, I was thinking. She should have been busying herself editing a *New Tales of Strange Events*.

Relating all those ghost stories invigorated my aunt. The newborn baby in the delivery room was still wailing when the nurse flung open the door, fuming mad, and said, "What kind of mother is that? She has her baby, dusts herself off, and runs away."

I cast a questioning glance at my aunt.

"She's the wife of a man from Black Water Village who's already had three children, all girls. She was hoping for a boy, but no such luck. And when her husband heard she'd had another girl, he simply drove off in his horse cart. Not the sort of father you see every day. Well, when she saw him run off like that, she jumped down off the delivery table, pulled up her pants, and ran out crying, leaving her new baby behind."

I followed my aunt into the delivery room to look at the newly abandoned baby. She was scrawny as a sickly kitten, nowhere as plump and healthy looking as the baby I'd found, and not nearly as cute; nor, for that matter, were her cries as robust. For some reason, that was a comforting thought.

My aunt poked her belly gently. "Slothful little thing," she said. "Why couldn't you grow one more little piece of meat? With it you'd have been the apple of their eye; without it you're nothing but an offensive little turd."

"What do we do with her?" the nurse asked. "We can't just leave her here, can we?"

My aunt turned to me. "Why don't you take her home with you? I've seen her parents, and there's nothing wrong with them. Tall, sturdy peasants, both of them. So this one ought to turn out just fine, maybe even a real beauty."

I was on my way out of the room before she'd even finished.

I sat in the sunflower field transfixed, my rear end and legs turning numb from the damp ground. I had no desire to stand up. The petals of the dish-shaped sunflowers had curled up and turned black, like eyelashes. Countless black, seedy eyes were staring at me. Dark cottony clouds blocked out the sun. The floral heads hung down in a state of disorder, as if in sad stupefaction. Black ants were busy rebuilding their tiny fortresses on the flat, muddy ground, making them taller and sturdier than the last time I'd seen them, oblivious to the reality that they would be leveled yet again the next time it rained, in utter disregard of the architectural history of their splendid ant kingdom. Lacking even a breath of wind, the sunflower field was oppressive as a kitchen steamer, in which a meaty, delectable duck — me — was being prepared.

Sitting there, I was reminded of something beautiful that had occurred in a big city somewhere: A beautiful, genteel young woman was in the habit of killing and eating young men. She braised their thighs, steamed their hips, and cooked their shredded hearts and livers in vinegar and garlic. Having devoured quite a few young men, the young woman was the picture of good health. Then I recalled something that had happened in China's distant past, right here in my own hometown: A chef by the name of Yi Ya cooked his own son and presented it to Duke Huan of Qi. They say that Yi Ya's son was incomparably delicious, far tastier than the tenderest lamb.

Those thoughts fortified my belief that human nature was more fragile than the thinnest paper. Just then, gusts of wind made the coarse sunflower leaves rustle coarsely as they brushed my head and face and, at the same time, rubbed against my pitted heart like sandpaper. I don't think I'd ever felt quite so comfortable. When the gusty wind died down, insects all around me burst forth with wonderful sounds. A small locust was riding on the back of a larger one next to a sunflower stalk; they were mating. In at least one significant way, they and humans are alike; that is to say, they are no more lowly than we, and we are no more noble than they. Nonetheless, hope was plentiful there in the sunflower field. Those drooping flowers were like countless children's faces, gazing at me affectionately, consoling me, and instilling me with the strength to come to grips with the world around me, no matter how painful that knowledge and understanding might be.

Unexpectedly, I was reminded of the conclusion to "Dolls of Michinoku." Once the author of the story understood the custom of drowning babies and had returned to Tokyo, he happened to see a row of marionettes, their eyes closed, hanging in a department store, coated with dust. The sight reminded him of all those babies who were cast into raging waters before they could open their eyes or cry for the first time. But I could find no such symbol on which to pin my sorrow and bring this chapter to an end. The sunflowers? The locusts? The ants? Crickets? Worms? Absurd, all of them. None of them represented the true face of life. In the tunnel I had dug for myself, I kept bumping into the white bones of abandoned children,

and I told myself that these human beings who filled the air
with sounds that might have been crying and might have been
laughter could not be viewed as unvirtuous or dishonest or
unlovely. Do the abandoned infants of Michinokou now belong to history? Condoms, IUDs, birth control pills, male and
female sterilization, and abortions have combined to eliminate
the cruel practice of drowning the infants of Michinokou.

And yet, here, in this place, where the land is blanketed
with yellow flowers, the issue is much more complex than that.
Doctors and the Township Government can work in concert to
force sterilization upon men and women of child-bearing age,
but where might we find a wonder drug capable of uprooting
and eliminating the petrified notions that cleave to the brains
of people in my hometown?